A WHAM Agency Library Mystery

The Case of the
Three-Legged Buffalo

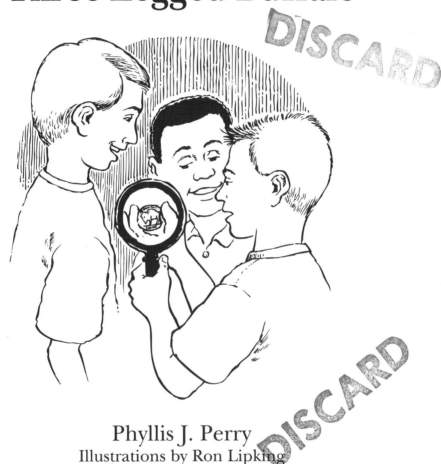

Phyllis J. Perry
Illustrations by Ron Lipking

Fort Atkinson, Wisconsin

For Emily.

Published by UpstartBooks
W5527 State Road 106
P.O. Box 800
Fort Atkinson, Wisconsin 53538-0800
1-800-448-4887

Copyright © 2006 by Phyllis J. Perry
Cover and interior illustrations © 2006 by Ron Lipking

The paper used in this publication meets the minimum requirements of American
National Standard for Information Science — Permanence of Paper for Printed
Library Material. ANSI/NISO Z39.48.

If I'd only had a new case to investigate, I'd never have done this—run for student council office, that is. My two fifth-grade buddies and I formed a private investigation agency a few weeks ago. We named it the WHAM Agency, using the letters from our names, Winklehockey, Aaron, and Mike (better known as Dynamike). Immediately we plunged into solving the case of a disappearing cat and discovering the owner of an old painting that we found in my flooded basement.

Although we'd been successful in solving both cases, and had handed out our business cards to everyone we met, there were no new cases. So when Mrs. Tilden said we should all seriously consider running for student council office, and Aaron and Dynamike reminded me how much I enjoyed being the banker when we played Monopoly®, I foolishly agreed to run for treasurer. And I'd won!

So here I was headed off to my first student council meeting. At least I was out of class for the rest of the afternoon. That meant I could put off deciding which U.S. president to pick for the subject of a short oral report I had to give in class on Friday. I'd look up some-body in the library later.

As I walked down the hall, I noticed an election poster that had been missed during cleanup. It still hung above the drinking fountain. Aaron, the brain, came up with the slogan, "Stop and think! Vote for Wink!" and Dynamike, the artist, did the zig-zaggity lightning designs for the posters. Pasted in the middle was my wallet-sized school photo that I hated. I wore a dumb smile, and my red cowlick looked like someone was holding up a finger behind my head. I pulled the poster off the wall, wadded it up, and tossed it in the trash.

"Wait up, Wink," a voice behind me called.

I turned and inwardly groaned when I saw Allison Parsley and Jo Miller hurrying to catch up with me. They were both in my fifth-grade homeroom. I had to admit that Jo was all right. We'd chosen her to be our room representative. But Allison was a royal pain. Too late I'd learned that she was running for office, or I'd have never run myself. Working with her as student council secretary would be about as much fun as having a toothache.

We hurried to Room 25, slipped inside, and took a seat. It was almost two o'clock and the council was gathering. After introductions, Mr. Doyle went over Robert's Rules of Order, or how to run a meeting.

"Each student council does something special for the school just before they turn things over to a new council," Mr. Doyle said. "The first semester group bought the clock that was just installed outside at the end of the school building. It's big and very useful, but it was expensive. Now we only have $3.11 left in the treasury."

4

When Mr. Doyle was finished, Brett Wallace, the new president, took over. Allison sat, pencil in hand, ready to record what happened next. I received a small metal cash box and key from the old treasurer. I put my hand on the box to protect it and felt really proud.

"Is there any new business?" Brett asked. His voice sounded a little funny, and he cleared his throat.

Jennifer Chen, the vice president, raised her hand. "I think we'd better come up with a fund-raiser idea right away," she said.

"Yeah," Brett agreed. "Anyone have an idea?"

Jo raised her hand. "There's a winter fair at the Elks' Club next weekend to raise money for the city orchestra. My mom's garden club is going to sell plants at the fair. Mom told me that any group can have a booth."

"I went last year," Jennifer said. "They sold all kinds of stuff—pottery, food, plants, jewelry. If we had something good to sell, we'd make tons of money."

"You pay five dollars for your booth and you put up a card table and sell things," Jo continued. "Twenty-five percent of your profit goes to the orchestra, and you get to keep the rest."

Brett turned to Mr. Doyle. "Could we do something like that?"

"Sure," Mr. Doyle said. "But if the fair is next weekend, it means moving fast. You'll have to call right away to get a booth, figure out what you're going to sell, and organize it all. Do you think you can do that in one week?"

"Sure," Allison said. "I'll call and reserve a space for us tonight." Leave it up to Allison to be the first to volunteer.

"But we don't even have five dollars in the treasury to pay the fee for the booth," Brett pointed out.

There was a gloomy silence during which I scribbled a math problem in my notebook and checked it twice.

"I'd be willing to loan the student council one dollar and eighty-nine cents to be paid back out of the profits of our sale," I offered. Hey, I could look like a hero, too, as long as it didn't cost much. At the moment, I had two dollars in my pocket.

"Great!" Brett said. "We'll put an I.O.U. in the money box and include it in the minutes of our meeting." Clearly Brett was getting the hang of this student council president thing. Allison began to scribble frantically.

"Okay," Mr. Doyle said. "You have someone calling to reserve the space, and you have your five dollar fee. Now, what are you going to sell?"

A third grader raised his hand. "We made some neat clay pots in art. Maybe we could sell those."

A fourth grader spoke. "It wouldn't be fair to just sell pots from the third grade. Every class should contribute, but how can every class get something ready by Friday?"

There was another gloomy silence. I concentrated hard, but drew a blank. Then as I stared at the table, I noticed the cover on the spiral notebook in front of the girl next to me. It had beagle puppies on it chewing a bone.

It made me think of my dog, Bugle. He loved to eat. Suddenly the idea hit. Forgetting all about Robert's Rules of Order, I shouted out, "Popcorn!"

Everyone liked the idea of selling popcorn, and Mr. Doyle said he'd loan us 20 dollars to cover expenses and give us change to start the sale. We were probably the only student council in the history of the school that had nothing in our treasury except two I.O.U.s.

As the meeting ended, I handed Brett Wallace one of our WHAM Agency cards. After all, as president, he had connections now. Maybe he'd have a need for our services.

Walking home from school, I gave Aaron and Dynamike an account of the first student council meeting.

"Selling popcorn at the fair's a great idea," Dynamike said. "How much?"

"Twenty-five cents a bag."

I knew the popcorn idea would appeal to Dynamike. He was the smallest kid in fifth grade, but he had the biggest appetite.

"Can we help?" Aaron asked. "Things have sure been quiet for the WHAM Agency. Nothing doing at all."

"Sure you guys can help," I said. "My job is to work at the table the first and last hour of the day. When the sale is over, I pick up all the money and figure out how much we made."

"That could take a while," Aaron said.

"Mr. Doyle said I could bring the cash box home and do my calculations over the weekend," I explained. "Then I'm supposed to hand over the report and the money to him at school on Monday morning. Want to come to the fair and then help me count the profits?"

"Sounds like fun," Dynamike said.

"Yeah," Aaron agreed.

Saturday morning, the three of us biked to the Elks' Club at the edge of town. When we arrived, the place was buzzing.

The fair was in the Elks' big ballroom. People were running around, putting up signs, and arranging stuff. It didn't take long to find Booth 63 in the middle of the north wall. Mr. Doyle was there, and kids were putting up decorations.

There was a big white sign taped to the front of the table that said "Hennessey School Fund Raiser" in small blue letters and "FRESH POPCORN—25¢" in giant red letters. Red, white, and blue helium balloons were tied to the back leg of the card table and floated above our booth.

"Ready for some change?" Mr. Doyle asked, as we came up.

"Ready," I said, and scooted behind the table where I quickly opened up the cash box with the key that I now wore on a chain around my neck. Mr. Doyle gave me ten dollars worth of quarters, dimes, nickels, and some one-dollar bills. I counted it all out and put it in my box. He also gave me a receipt for the supplies. Behind me,

Brett Wallace was working away. I heard the first pop-pop-pop from the air popper and sniffed.

"Smells as if you're ready for business," Dynamike said hopefully.

"Not quite," Mr. Doyle said. "We have to fill the bags."

Just then Jennifer came hurrying up. Aaron and Dynamike left to scope out the fair. They promised they'd come back to buy later.

I was surprised at the crowd. As soon as the doors opened, people poured in. My friend Mrs. Carabell, who had been the first client of the WHAM Agency, came with one of her friends and bought our first bag of popcorn.

Two people popped, salted, and bagged the popcorn behind us. Jennifer took orders and handed out bags to customers. I took money and made change.

Right at ten o'clock, Aaron and Dynamike came to get me. All three of us bought a bag of popcorn before I turned the booth over to the next student council team.

"There's a lot of neat stuff for sale here," Dynamike said.

"Great, 'cause I have to find a birthday present for my mom," I said. "I've got just over eight dollars to spend."

We walked along, munching popcorn as we looked. There was tons of jewelry, but most of it was pretty expensive. I found some earrings on sale for five dollars, but they were for pierced ears, and my mom doesn't wear that kind. There was lots of artsy-craftsy stuff, but most of it didn't appeal to me.

We kept looking. Wayside Pottery had two tables, and on one of them there were coffee mugs for eight dollars, tax included. Bingo! Mom loved her breakfast coffee—now to zero in on the perfect mug.

"Are you looking for something in particular?" asked the young woman in the booth. She was dressed in a bright tie-dyed shirt and had one long braid hanging down her back.

"Yeah," I said. "I need something really unusual. A mug that stands out from all the rest."

The young woman laughed. "I may have what you want," she said. She reached into a box for a mug and set it on the counter. "What do you think?"

The mug stood out all right. It was shaped like a round body with no head, and only one arm curved into a handle. It stood on legs ending in two, big, bare clay feet, complete with toes and toenails that held the mug about two inches off the table.

"Perfect!" I said. "My mom will love it." Dynamike looked a little doubtful, and I could tell from the expression on Aaron's face that he didn't agree at all. But they didn't know my mom. This mug would be one of her prized possessions. Big Feet. I could hardly wait to give it to her. I noticed the woman tucked a Wayside Pottery card in with the mug, so I handed her our business card, too. You never can tell when someone might need an investigation agency.

By the time I closed the booth at six o'clock, the cash box was filled with bills and heavy with coins. Dynamike, Aaron, and I went home to eat and then an hour later, gathered back at my house. We went downstairs to my rec room where I'd put the cash box, some envelopes, and a pad and pencil. I took the chain off my neck and used the key to unlock the box.

"First," I said, "let's separate the money. Then we can do the counting."

"Good plan," Aaron said, and he started making piles of bills while Dynamike and I separated the coins into heaps.

"Hey! Here's a ten!" Aaron said. "A big spender!"

"Great," I said, "that'll cover the ten dollars worth of change Mr. Doyle gave us to get started." I put the ten dollars in a separate envelope with his I.O.U. inside and wrote Mr. Doyle's name on the front.

"And here's another I.O.U." Aaron unfolded it and read, "Student Council owes Wink $1.89."

I put that I.O.U. with $1.89 in another envelope, wrote my name on it, and made a note on my pad.

"Now we have to take out the expense money for the popcorn, balloons, and stuff. Let's see," I pulled out some receipts from Mr. Doyle. "Expenses are $10.50."

Aaron handed me two fives and Dynamike gave me fifty cents. I put that money in a third marked envelope and entered the amount on my pad.

"Now we count up the rest and set 25 percent aside for our donation to the orchestra. Everything else will be profit. How about stacking the coins in dollar piles?" I suggested.

Dynamike set the quarters in piles of four while Aaron made piles of ten dimes, and I made piles of 20 nickels. Thomas Jefferson, whose head was on many of the nickels, began to look pretty familiar to me. While I was counting, I decided that I might as well write my president report on him. When I suddenly came upon an Indian head nickel, I stopped to take a look at it.

"Hmmm," I said, turning it over. "It's a great looking Indian, but how come the buffalo on the back only has three legs? If I were making the design for millions of coins, I'd be sure to put all four legs on the buffalo."

"Let me see that!" Aaron said. He grabbed the coin and stared hard at it.

"It is a three-legged buffalo." There was no mistaking the excitement in his voice. "Wink, I think the WHAM Agency has a brand-new mystery on its hands. How did a nickel like this get spent on popcorn at the fair? Do you know how much this coin is worth?"

2

"Yeah, I know how much it's worth. A nickel's worth five cents," I said firmly while looking Aaron straight in the eye. I wasn't about to lose any part of our student council profits. "The fact that it's defective and that this buffalo only has three legs isn't our fault. We gave fresh, hot popcorn for it. A nickel's a nickel."

"No," Aaron said. "You don't get it. If this nickel is genuine, it's worth a lot more than a nickel. I think we've got a valuable coin here."

"You mean we're rich?" Dynamike asked.

"I'm not an expert," Aaron said, "but you guys know that I collect coins and read a lot about them. I'm even a member of the American Numismatic Association."

"Mumis-what?" I asked.

"I didn't know you were asthmatic," Dynamike said. He looked confused.

"Not asthmatic. Numismatic." Aaron rolled his eyes. "A numismatist is someone who collects coins. My dad collects coins, too, and he gets magazines and newspapers like *Coin World* and *Error Trends*. He reads about coins all the time."

I remembered a visit to Aaron's house months earlier. "Yeah. He showed me a special penny once. He was pretty excited about it."

"Dad's really interested in mint errors," Aaron said. "Sometimes the mint makes a mistake. As soon as the workers notice a mistake, of course, they fix it. But sometimes some of the coins with mistakes slip through and get into circulation. They're rare and worth a lot to collectors. I'm pretty sure I've heard Dad talk about a three-legged buffalo."

"Wow!" I said. "So this nickel might be valuable to a coin collector?"

"You've got it!" Aaron grinned.

"Sounds like a case for the WHAM Agency," I said.

"You mean we investigate to find out how much it's worth?" Dynamike asked.

"Yeah," I said. "And where it came from. And who spent it. And if they know it's part of a valuable coin collection. And whether or not we can keep it. Seems like there's a lot to investigate to me."

"Before we start investigating, we'd better finish adding up the money and do the report," suggested Aaron. "Then I'll call my dad and ask him about the three-legged buffalo."

I was inspired now and wanted to get this report out of the way and start on solving a new mystery. So there wasn't much talking as we quickly completed the dollar piles and examined the coins.

Each one of us took a sheet of paper and added up all the money that hadn't been put in marked envelopes. Then we compared figures. It didn't surprise me when we didn't agree the first time and had to do it over again. Finally we all came up with the same number, $76, which, of course, was what Aaron had the first time.

"So, after taking out money to replace the change we borrowed," I said, "and deducting the expenses for renting table space and buying supplies, we made $76, of which we have to give the orchestra $19. So our profit is $57."

I wrote up the report. "Hey, pretty good," I said. "Our student council treasury isn't so pitiful any more."

"How many bags of popcorn did you sell?" asked Dynamike.

I groaned. Another delay.

"The kids will want to know," Dynamike insisted.

"Here, give me a piece of paper," Aaron said. Quickly he scribbled some numbers. "You can report that the student council sold 366 bags of popcorn."

I didn't argue or even check the figures. Aaron doesn't make mistakes. I just wrote it down in my report.

"Now," I said, "We can start work on the Case of the Three-Legged Buffalo!" I shoved all the coins except the Indian head nickel back into the cash box, put the envelopes and the report on top, and locked it up. Then we scrambled up the stairs to the phone.

"Hey! What's the rush?" my dad asked, as we came charging into the kitchen. "You guys act like you're being chased by wild animals."

"You're close," I said. "The WHAM Agency is on the job again. This time it's the Case of the Three-Legged Buffalo."

"A three-legged buffalo?" said Mom, walking into the kitchen.

"Yeah, I just found one," I explained.

"In our basement?" asked Mom. "I hope it's house-broken."

I smiled at Mom's lame joke. "Aaron," I said, "why don't you call your dad now?" While Aaron dialed his number, I showed the nickel to my mom and dad.

"Well, would you look at that," Dad said, holding it to the light. "It is missing a leg." Then my mom took a turn examining it.

By this time, Aaron had his father on the phone. "My dad said he'd be happy to look at the nickel. He wants to know if he should come over, or if we want to go over to my house."

"Invite him to come over here," Mom said. "I'll make us a pot of coffee."

A few minutes later, Mr. Bates was at the front door. Like Aaron, he was tall, skinny, and blonde. He had a couple of books tucked under his arm.

"Let's see this valuable coin," he said, as he headed for the living room.

I handed Mr. Bates the nickel. He walked to the lamp on the end table and held it close to the light. Then he pulled a magnifying glass out of his jacket pocket and took a closer look.

"Whew!" he finally said. "It looks authentic. Of course, you'd need to have that confirmed by a dealer. Sometimes people file off a leg, trying to make the coin valuable. But this one's got all the right markings. There's the 1937 Denver mint mark. It's got some little dots right under the belly. And you can see where the fourth leg should be between the foot and the fur at the top."

None of us had noticed all that, so we all crowded around him. "Here," Mr. Bates said, "why don't you each take a turn?" He set the coin on the table and handed the magnifying glass to me. I looked and then passed it to Dynamike.

Mom served coffee to the grown-ups, and I brought cans of soda pop for Aaron, Dynamike, and me. When Mom passed around a plate of her peanut butter cookies, I watched Dynamike's eyes brighten. I didn't know how much our nickel was worth, but I knew that Dynamike would have traded it for a plate of my mom's cookies any day.

"How did a three-legged buffalo get on a nickel?" I asked.

"It was a mistake," Mr. Bates said. "I've heard about the three-legged buffalo, of course. Every collector has. It's a pretty famous coin. But after Aaron phoned, I looked it up in Breen's Encyclopedia."

"What's that?" asked Dynamike.

"It's a coin encyclopedia," Mr. Bates said.

"You mean there's a special encyclopedia just for coins?" I asked.

"Sure," Mr. Bates said. "And it explained that this mistake is the result of what's called die clashing. That's pretty common in any mint."

"Die clashing?"

"Yeah," Aaron said. "I know what that means. A die is like a stamp. To stamp the pictures on the coins, you use two dies, one for the front and one for the back. If the machine gets jammed, a blank coin doesn't slip into place. Then the two dies strike each other."

"Right," Aaron's dad said. "This may happen several times until someone notices the problem."

"Then what happens?" Dynamike asked.

"Normally," Mr. Bates said. "The pressman stops the press, discards the damaged dies, puts on new ones, and starts operating again. But my encyclopedia explains that in 1937 when this accident occurred, a new pressman named Mr. Young was working. He was trying to impress people by working fast. So instead of replacing the clashed dies, he took an emery stick and ground off the clash marks. Then he went right on printing nickels."

"So Mr. Young accidentally filed off the leg," Aaron said.

"Right," Mr. Bates said. "But he didn't know it. Those coins moved right into sealed sacks with the normal ones before the inspectors noticed. From the mint sacks, they went to branch banks and out to the public."

"How many of these three-legged buffalo nickels got made?" I asked.

"No one is sure," Mr. Bates said.

"How much is it worth?" Dynamike asked.

"Depends on the condition," Aaron said. "Coins are graded from fair to very fine and uncirculated."

"What makes a coin fair or fine?" Dynamike wanted to know.

"Uncirculated coins are the most valuable. They've got a bright finish. But when coins are used, they bang around against other coins in people's pockets and in cash registers. Parts of the design wear off. An expert would have to grade our nickel."

"What sorts of things will an expert look for?" I asked.

"I guess an expert would look at the Indian's cheekbones and feathers, and the detail on the buffalo's horn or tail to see if they're worn," Aaron said.

His father nodded. "Nickel metal is hard," Mr. Bates added, "and when you get a high-relief design, some of the coins aren't well struck to begin with. Parts of the design are lightly impressed and wear away fast. Of course, others get sharply struck. Then it depends what happens to the coin as it circulates."

"Can you give us some idea from your books of what our nickel's worth?" I asked.

Aaron flipped through the pages of the book his father had brought over. "In good condition," Aaron said, "my book says it's worth $80. In fine condition, $125."

"Wow!" I said. "That's more than we made on the whole popcorn sale."

"Who would spend a valuable coin like that just for a bag of popcorn?" Dynamike asked.

"That's what we need to find out," Aaron said. "Of course, it could be an accident. This coin may have been circulating and no one noticed. Someone might have had it in his pocket and pulled it out with a couple of dimes to buy a bag of popcorn."

"But what if some little kid, who didn't know how valuable a coin collection was, helped himself at home to a bunch of coins that he shouldn't be into and is spending them?" Dynamike said.

"Then I guess we'd have to return it, if we could," I said. "Finding out all about that nickel is a job for the WHAM Agency."

"We'd better look at the other coins," Aaron suggested.

"Yeah," I agreed. "There may be more valuable ones. I noticed that some of the pennies are sort of green. Does that mean they're valuable?"

"No," Aaron said. "It's easy for copper to turn green, and it sure doesn't add to the value of a coin."

"The cash box with all the coins is out in the kitchen," I said. "We could all pitch in and look for valuable coins if you can tell us what to look for."

"The first thing to look at is the dates," Aaron said. "Most of the coins will be later than 1980. Those are just worth their face value. If they're dated in the 1950s or earlier, let's pull them out and ask my dad to take a closer look at them."

"Good plan," Mr. Bates agreed. "Most coins dated in the '40s and '50s won't have much extra value either. But if you were to turn up a 1916 dime or a 1909 penny, you'd have something. Even the 1950 Denver mint nickel is worth about seven dollars."

We all trooped out into the kitchen. I used my key to unlock the cash box while my dad went to get a couple of magnifying glasses. We all arranged ourselves around the kitchen table. I dumped all the coins out in the middle. The grown-ups used the magnifiers and Dynamike, Aaron, and I used our sharp eyes to check out the dates.

I pounced on every nickel I could see, but old Mr. Jefferson was on every one of them. And Aaron was right. Almost all the coins were more recent than 1980.

"Hey," I yelled. "Here's a 1940 nickel. How much is it worth?"

Mr. Bates consulted the premium list in the book. "I hate to tell you this, Wink," he said, "but it's worth five cents."

"How come a coin that old isn't worth more?" I asked.

"Well, according to my book, they made 176,499,158 nickels that year in Philadelphia," Mr. Bates said. "When they make that many, the coin doesn't have a special value."

Even though there were six of us, it took quite a while to go through all the coins. The best we came up with was a wartime silver nickel, 1943 Denver mint. In extremely fine condition, it would be worth 15 cents.

And Mr. Bates said it was so worn, he thought it was only worth five cents.

"Well, that's it," I said, as we scooped up all the coins and put them back in the cash box.

"No more valuable coins," Aaron said. "Looks like that nickel was just a lucky accident."

"Maybe," I said. "But I have this funny feeling that the WHAM Agency isn't finished yet with the Case of the Three-Legged Buffalo."

3

"Should we hire an armored car to take you to school this morning, Wink?" Dad teased at breakfast. He must have seen me fingering the key on the chain around my neck and glancing often at the cash box on the kitchen counter.

I laughed. "No, thanks. Dynamike and Aaron make pretty good bodyguards. I think our student council profits will be safe."

Sure enough, on the way to school, as if they really were bodyguards, Aaron walked on one side of me and Dynamike on the other while I carried the cash box.

I could hardly wait to tell Mr. Doyle about the rare coin that turned up in our popcorn money. I had left the Indian head nickel at home where it would be safe, but the sales report was safely tucked in my notebook in my backpack.

"What do you think Mr. Doyle will say?" Dynamike asked as we hurried up the front walk of the school.

"I think he's going to be surprised that a nickel is worth more than a hundred bucks," I said. "I just hope that he thinks it's okay for us to keep it."

"My dad can't decide what to think," Aaron said. "Part of the time he says it's just one of those lucky accidents. And then the next minute he wonders out loud if some kid might be raiding his parents' coin collection. It's driving him nuts."

"Remind him that the WHAM Agency is on the job. We'll keep him posted," I said.

We walked right up to the front door of the school and straight to Mr. Doyle's fifth-grade classroom. Normally kids aren't supposed to enter the school building in the morning until the bell rings, but since we were carrying the cash box and obviously on a mission, no one stopped to question us.

"Hi, Mr. Doyle," I said, walking into his room.

"I'll bet you've got the money and the report on the popcorn sale." Mr. Doyle rose from his seat and walked over to a locked file cabinet that stood right behind his desk. He took a key and unlocked it. Then he reached for the cash box.

"Yeah," I said.

"How much did we make?"

"We added up the costs and the cash, and we made a profit of more than $50," I said, handing the report and cash box over to him. "But we also found a coin among the change that might be valuable."

"Really?" Mr. Doyle set the cash box down, picked up the report, and turned to look at us.

Before I could launch into telling him about the three-legged buffalo nickel, a voice came over the school intercom.

"Mr. Doyle? Would you report to the principal's office right away, please. Mr. Tobias needs a word with you before classes begin."

Mr. Doyle walked to the intercom button, pressed it, and said, "Be right there." Mr. Doyle ran his fingers through his thick salt-and-pepper hair. He looked rushed and nervous. Maybe teachers didn't like to report to the office any more than kids did.

"Wish I could stick around and talk with you guys about this, but I've got to run," he said. He set my report on top of the cash box and locked the cabinet. "How about coming in tomorrow morning ... no, wait." He looked back at his desk calendar. "I've got an appointment tomorrow before school. Tell you what, Wink, meet me here on Wednesday morning, and we'll go through your report, line by line, okay? And we'll discuss this strange coin you found." As he said this, he made a note on his calendar, then quickly headed for the door.

"Okay." I followed him out and watched him stride down the hall toward the office.

"Darn!" Dynamike said.

The three of us walked down the hall in the opposite direction and out the back door to the playground. I felt deflated. Maybe I should have spoken up and told Mr. Doyle this was super important and the principal could wait.

"We'd better keep the three-legged buffalo a secret until after we meet with Mr. Doyle," I said.

No sooner had this come out of my mouth than Allison and Jo came walking over to us. Something looked different about Allison that I couldn't quite put my finger on. Suddenly I realized what it was. I could see her eyes. Usually her long bangs hung over them. She must have gotten a haircut.

"Hello, Moneybags," Allison said. "How much did we make on the popcorn sale?"

"Our profit is over $50," I bragged.

"Great!" Jo said.

"How many bags of popcorn did we sell?" Allison wanted to know.

I looked at Dynamike. He had a grin on his face. "Told ya' they'd ask," he said under his breath.

"We sold 366 bags," I said.

"Guess it'll be an exciting student council meeting next Friday when I bring up the big news!" Allison said.

I was already walking away, but when she punched those last two words, I stopped in my tracks. Big news? Had the information about the three-legged buffalo leaked out? "What big news?" I asked, glancing at Aaron and Dynamike.

"Should we tell?" Allison asked Jo.

"Why not? Everybody'll know about it Friday anyway," Jo pointed out, "and the more student council members who've thought about it ahead of time, the better. If lots of kids like the idea, we'll get it passed."

"My idea for another fund-raiser is a carnival!" Allison spoke fast. Clearly she had to talk or she would pop.

"I'm suggesting the student council sponsor a school carnival in the gym."

"Every class and club can have a booth with games to play and prizes for winners," Jo added. "It'll be free to get in, but you'll have to pay to get tickets to play the games. There'll be games for grown-ups and for kids. You know, like darts, beanbag throw, ring toss, that kind of stuff."

"All the profits will go to student council," Allison said with a smirk. "I'll bet we can make a lot more than the $60 we made off of your popcorn sale idea."

So that was it. Allison couldn't swallow the fact that somebody besides her had come up with a suggestion for making money for the student council. She had to top it with something bigger and better. I folded my arms in front of me and stuck out my chin. Well, I wasn't voting for her crazy carnival.

"The prizes to give away at all the booths will cost quite a bit of money, won't they?" Aaron asked. "That'll cut into the profits."

I had to give him credit. Aaron always listens to an idea, thinks about it, and checks out the possibilities no matter who suggests it. That's why I know he's going to be the CEO of a big corporation and make a bundle one day.

"We're hoping that some local businesses might donate the prizes," Jo said. "Then we can list them as sponsors in the flyers we'll spread around the neighborhood. It'd be good advertising for them."

"Hmmm! Might work," Aaron said.

"Will there be any food?" Dynamike asked.

I stared at my two buddies. Traitors! Why were they being so supportive of an idea that came from Allison Parsley? Couldn't they see she was just trying to top my idea?

"Who knows?" Allison said airily. "Maybe a class will want to sell popcorn. But that's such a worn-out idea. I'm hoping that our class will come up with something a little more original."

That last comment really made me mad, but I managed to keep my mouth shut. I just glared at her, turned, and walked off.

Aaron and Dynamike followed me. Dynamike must have finally tuned in to how I was feeling. Glancing back over his shoulder, he yelled, "Fads like short skirts and short bangs come and go. But some things, like apple pie and hot popcorn, are never out of style."

Dynamike's parting shot, particularly the comment about Allison's new bangs, made me feel a lot better. I grinned at him and slugged him in the shoulder.

"Way to go!" Aaron punched his other shoulder.

"Old Allison won't be the only one with big news on Friday," I whispered. "Wait 'til the kids hear about the three-legged buffalo."

The bell rang, and during Language Arts, after we'd worked on our new spelling words for a while, Mrs. Tilden said, "Class!" to get our attention. And then she turned on her brightest smile.

I'd come to be suspicious of that smile. It meant she'd hatched a wonderful idea that would somehow translate into a lot of work for us. Inwardly I groaned, because right now I had plenty on my mind and didn't need any new challenges.

"All of you have shown improvement in your writing," she said. "It's fun to read your short stories. You've written mysteries, adventures, and some fantastic science fiction."

I wondered if she could be referring to my last great story, "Up on Mars."

"In our new assignment," Mrs. Tilden continued, "I'm hoping you'll find out that truth is even stranger than fiction. Your next writing assignment won't be to invent a story. Instead, I'm going to ask you to dig up some really interesting facts to share with us." The smile got brighter.

I looked at Dynamike, who turned his head and wiggled his eyebrows at me. Whatever assignment Mrs. Tilden dreamed up, Aaron, the brain, would have no trouble with it. He'd turn in a dream assignment. But Dynamike and I spotted a nightmare ahead. Digging up facts sounded like a lot of work.

Mrs. Tilden continued, "I want you to choose something that you're really interested in. You might use our school library or the city library to learn more about it. All your information doesn't need to come from books; you can interview people, or you might watch a special videotape on your subject."

"Then you'll write your report and share it orally with the class. Here's an assignment sheet with all the details." Mrs. Tilden took a stack of papers from her desk and started handing them out to us.

"We'll spend several class periods researching in the library. But I'll be expecting you to put in some home-work time, too. Any questions?"

I saw Allison signaling Jo that they'd work together. Jo nodded and Allison's hand shot up immediately. "Can we work with a partner?"

I had to admit that was a smart question. If she could team up with Jo, she'd have it made. For that matter, I was planning to work with Aaron and Dynamike.

"Not this time," Mrs. Tilden said.

I joined in a loud groan that rose from the class.

"It's a short report. Only two pages. So I want each person to write one. Any more questions?" She waited, but no more hands went up.

"All right," she went on. "At the bottom of the assign-ment page, there's a tear-off piece. Once you've selected your topic, fill out that part and give it to me. I'd like each of you to select a topic by Wednesday."

By Wednesday! I groaned again. How could I make progress on a new case if Mrs. Tilden's assignment was going to eat up all my time? Last night I'd been plan-ning what the WHAM Agency had to do, starting this afternoon. We had places to go and people to see. Then Mr. Doyle ran out on me and slowed us down, and now this.

"Remember, don't pick a topic that's too big. You can't write about Transportation in two pages, but you could write about Henry Ford's first car."

I squirmed. I wasn't worrying about choosing a topic that was too big. I was worrying about coming up with any topic at all.

"Take the rest of this period before lunch to discuss ideas with your friends," Mrs. Tilden continued. "Have them help you narrow your idea down to something you can handle."

A buzz broke out immediately as kids dragged chairs around, and small knots of friends got together to talk about the assignment. Dynamike and I joined Aaron at the back of the room.

Dynamike looked as glum as I felt. Aaron, as usual, seemed excited about the new idea.

"I wish we could work together," Dynamike complained. "Then it wouldn't be so bad."

"Well, Mrs. Tilden says we can't," Aaron pointed out. "So that's that. Now let's do some thinking."

I sat there, the fingers of one hand drumming on my desk, while my other hand, in my pocket, fingered my lunch money. I wasn't thinking about my report. I was planning the next steps in our case and wishing it was noon so I could escape. Then suddenly an idea hit. Pure inspiration!

"Hey!" I whispered. "I've got a great idea."

4

"What's your idea?" Dynamike asked, leaning in closer from his desk.

"Two for the price of one," I said smugly. Then I lowered my voice. "We have to do some research for the WHAM Agency anyway. So why not write our school reports on coins? We can use the same books. We can all interview Aaron's dad. And we can talk to people in the coin shops, too."

"Genius," Dynamike whispered back. He grinned broadly. "We can work together after all." He gave me a friendly poke in the shoulder. "And since you came up with it, I think you should get to do your report on the three-legged buffalo."

"I'd sure like to," I said.

"Then you should," Aaron agreed. "And I already know which coin I want to write on, the 1928 Indian head nickel. My dad said no one even noticed it until 1960, but it's another one of those strange things that happened in the mint. They punched a D mint mark over an S mark. It's the first time a coin was discovered with two mint marks."

"Well, if you guys are both writing about nickels, I will too," said Dynamike. "I'll find out about the Jefferson nickels. Okay? They may not be rare or very valuable, but everybody has seen them and handled them a lot, so I think kids would be interested in them."

"Perfect. That way any books we can find on nickels will help all of us," I said. "And it'll be a good cover while we're working on our new case. This way we don't have to wait until we've talked to Mr. Doyle to be asking questions about the three-legged buffalo. If anyone, like snoopy Allison, hears that we're asking around about nickels, no one will guess we're trying to find out about a rare coin from the popcorn sale. It will seem like we're just working on our school report."

Dynamike and I pushed our desks back into their regular places, and all three of us started filling in the information on the bottom of our assignment pages. I finished mine first and took it up to Mrs. Tilden's desk. Dynamike and Aaron were right behind me.

"Well, you boys work fast," Mrs. Tilden said, taking the slip from me. "Let's see, Wink, you'll be researching the 1937 Indian head nickel. Now, that's an unusual topic. I didn't know you were a numismatist."

"I'm not," I admitted, kind of proud that I even knew what the word meant. "But now that I've become the student council treasurer, I've taken a greater interest in coins."

She gave me a puzzled look before turning to reach up for Dynamike's slip and reading it. "And Dynamike, you're going to find out about the Jefferson nickel?"

"Uh-huh," Dynamike said.

"All right," Mrs. Tilden agreed. She reached for Aaron's slip. "Let me guess," she said, without looking at the paper. "You're going to find out about a nickel, too."

Then she looked down at his slip and said, "Hmmm. The 1938 double-mint-mark nickel. Well, boys, I can see that our class is going to learn a lot about nickels in the next few weeks. Good luck."

I gave a little sigh of relief. For a teacher, Mrs. Tilden was pretty reasonable.

During lunch, Aaron, Dynamike, and I talked about our new case. I pulled out the notebook and stubby pencil I always kept in my back pocket and made a list. Quickly, I jotted down three things. 1) Look up coin shops to get their addresses. 2) Take our nickel in for appraisal. 3) Clear with Mr. Doyle whether or not we could sell the nickel we found in the popcorn sale money.

I felt good as I was writing. Ideas I had floating around in my head were just that, ideas. But when they were written down, I had a plan.

That night after dinner, Dynamike and I went over to Aaron's house. We'd agreed that was the best place to start our research, with his dad. Aaron led us straight to the dining room where his dad sat. Books and magazines were stacked on the table. Mr. Bates was expecting us, and from the way he smiled, I was sure that he was glad we came.

"Hello, boys," Mr. Bates said. "I think it's great that you're going to do research reports on coins. Who knows? You may all get hooked and become collectors! Your student council sponsor is in for a shock when you tell him about your nickel. I've done a little market research since I last saw you, and the price on that nickel has gone way up."

"It has?" I asked. "How much is it worth?"

"Well," Mr. Bates said, "the other night when I came over, I looked up your nickel in what we call the Red Book and the Blue Book. The Red Book is a list of United States coins and their current value. The Blue Book lists dealer buying prices."

"Wouldn't they be the same?" Dynamike asked.

"No," Aaron put in. "You see, dealers pay a lot less than the coin will sell for. They have to price it low and sell it higher so that they pay their overhead and make a profit."

"My books were a couple of years old," Mr. Bates continued. "But this afternoon, I bought the most recent editions, and I was surprised." He handed the new books over to us. "Why don't you take a look?" Aaron took one book and Dynamike and I took the other.

Aaron knew how to use these books and he quickly found the listing in both books for our three-legged buffalo nickel. He ran his finger across the sheets at the values. His face broke into a big grin. "Wow!" he said. "A couple of years have made quite a difference!"

Mr. Bates smiled. "Right. If your coin is in really good condition, it's worth a lot. Of course, a dealer will have to grade it. Since a buyer would pay $250 for a coin in extra fine condition, you may be able to get $200 or more from a dealer for that nickel!"

I let out a whistle. It sounded too good to be true.

"But before you get your hopes up," Mr. Bates went on, and his smile faded as his face turned serious, "in the past, dishonest people have filed off one of the legs from an ordinary nickel and tried to sell it as a three-legged one. So it could be a fake. Then it's only worth five cents. A dealer will let you know for sure."

I caught the frown on Dynamike's face. I was worried, too. It was going to be an awful letdown if that nickel was a fake.

"Now, what are the WHAM Agency's next steps?" Mr. Bates asked. His smile had returned, and he looked eager.

"We have some ideas," I said. "After school, I looked up coins in the yellow pages of our phone book and made some notes." I pulled my trusty notebook out of my back pocket. Right behind the to-do list, I'd written down some names and addresses.

"There are two coin shops listed right here in town and four others in neighboring towns. I thought we'd go visit the local shops tomorrow after school and find out as much as we can. Then we'd have that information to share with Mr. Doyle on Wednesday morning."

"Great!" Mr. Bates said. "I've used the local coin shops. They're both authorized dealers for the American Numismatic Society. That's important, because it means you can trust them to give you a fair value. I hope you'll keep me posted on your progress. Now, do you have any questions to ask about your reports?"

We spent about two hours looking through books and magazines. We took notes and asked Mr. Bates questions. I found myself smiling. At first I'd dreaded these research papers. But I found out that if you were researching something you were really interested in, it was a lot of fun.

>—+—◆◇—·—○—◇◆—+—≺

Right after school on Tuesday, we biked downtown. The first coin shop was tiny. The man behind the counter who greeted us was plump and had lots of white hair. With a fake beard, he'd be good at playing Santa Claus. When he heard what we wanted, he was polite, but he admitted nickels weren't his specialty.

"I work mostly in gold, medallions, silver dollars, and currency," he said. He pointed to a nearby wall. It, like the other walls of his shop, was lined with picture frames containing series of paper money.

"Look at all those pictures of George," Dynamike whispered, pointing to a one-dollar series. "Those are the only portraits I've ever seen that I'd really like to have on my bedroom wall. They'd look great next to my football poster." But when he got close enough to read the prices, Dynamike sighed. Sets of special dollar bills don't come cheap.

The second address was in a shopping center at the north end of town. When we got there, we found the shop was big and lined with glass cases. In the back we could see the door of what seemed to be an enormous walk-in safe. There were display racks everywhere. You pushed a button and a tray of coins moved up into sight at the top. Then if you pushed the button again, another tray came up, sort of like a tiny Ferris wheel. When the man finished waiting on a customer, he turned to us.

"Can I help you boys?" he asked, and smiled.

I liked him right away. He treated us like regular customers. I've seen a lot of shop clerks who took one look and ignored me, obviously hoping I'd leave and not take up their valuable time. Some clerks seemed to think I was just another pesky kid good for nothing but leaving finger marks on spotless glass counters.

"We'd like to know how much you'd give us for this," I said, as I reached into my pocket and pulled out the coin that now rested in the small plastic case Aaron's dad had given us.

"What have we got here?" the man asked, as he carefully unwrapped the coin.

"A three-legged buffalo," I said.

He turned on a bright light, put a velvet pad on the counter, and laid the nickel on it. Then he picked up a jeweler's loupe and took a long, hard look.

I dug my hands in my pockets and found myself holding my breath as I waited.

After a very long time in which he kept turning it over and bringing it up close to the glass, he finally looked at me and said, "It's genuine and in good shape. It's worth quite a bit of money."

I exhaled and felt the grin spreading across my face. Dynamike and Aaron gave each other high fives.

"May I ask where you got it?" the dealer asked.

"Someone spent it for a bag of popcorn at our student council sale," I replied truthfully. "Whatever it's worth will go into the Hennessey School student council treasury."

"How much money did you make on the popcorn sale?" the clerk asked.

"After expenses, around 50 dollars," I said.

"Well, you've just upped your student council profit considerably. I'd rate this as almost uncirculated, a 50 on the scale we use to rate coins. Let me see here." He flipped through the pages of a coin magazine on the counter.

"I'll be able to sell it for about $365. There's quite a demand for these. As a matter of fact, I don't have another in stock. Sold my last one Saturday. So it won't last long. Let me figure out the price I'd pay you."

My ears perked up. He'd just sold a three-legged buffalo? What a strange coincidence. I wished I had the nerve to ask who he'd sold one to on Saturday. But I reminded myself that it wasn't very likely that someone would come in and buy a valuable coin and then rush right out and spend it on a bag of popcorn.

The coin dealer picked up a calculator from a desk behind the counter and did some quick figuring. "I pay 35 percent less than the selling price. That's $237.25. Since it's for your student council, I'll offer you an even $250 for your nickel. Deal?"

"I can let you know real soon," I said. "We're meeting with our school sponsor tomorrow morning. I wanted to tell him how much it's worth before we make a decision about selling it."

"Fair enough. Let me give you my name," the man said. "I'm Bob Jennings." He reached over the counter to shake my hand.

"Carlton Winklehockey," I said. "Everyone calls me Wink. And this is Aaron and Dynamike." He shook hands with them, too.

"Well, here's my card, boys." As he handed each of us his card, I quickly reached in my back pocket and handed him our WHAM Agency card in return.

He read it with a slightly puzzled look on his face and tucked it in his shirt pocket. "Give me a call after you talk with your sponsor. Is there anything else I can help you with?"

"If you're not too busy," Aaron said, "I wonder if you have a 1938 D over S that we could look at. We're not going to buy it," he hastened to say. "But I'm writing a report for class and I'd like to actually see one."

"No problem," Mr. Jennings said. He went into the vault and came back with a small piece of white cardboard in his hand. A coin with a thin, clear film over it fit snugly in the center. In the upper right-hand corner was written 1938D/S. In the left corner was the rating: XF. And in the bottom corner was the price: $100.

Mr. Jennings said, "This one's in extra fine condition." He handed over the loupe. "Hold this close to your eye, and then bring the coin up to it until you can see clearly."

As Aaron maneuvered the coin and the glass, Mr. Jennings said, "If you look closely, you'll see just a little of the top loop of the S above the D and a piece of the bottom loop behind it. You can also see a piece of the S in the middle of the D."

"I can see it!" Aaron said. "Clear as anything."

We each took a turn with the loupe.

"How about you?" Mr. Jennings turned to Dynamike. "Are you into nickels, too?"

"Yes, sir," Dynamike said. "I'm doing my report on Jefferson nickels, but I know they're not very valuable."

"Not so," Mr. Jennings said. He smiled. "Come over here." He walked Dynamike to one of the revolving cases and pulled up a tray. "Here are the earliest Jefferson nickels. The first was in 1938." He reached in, took out a cardboard square, and handed it to Dynamike. "Take a look."

Dynamike held the coin and looked at the price in the lower corner. "You mean this nickel costs $120?" he asked. "That's more than the strike-over one."

"Right," Mr. Jennings said, "because it's a proof coin, made in Philadelphia. See how bright and sharp it is? Proof coins are purchased at the mint for a premium."

We all took a look. A customer walked in then, so Dynamike thanked Mr. Jennings and handed back the nickel. We all said good-bye.

"I'll be calling you," I promised.

"How about that," Dynamike said, shaking his head when we were outside the store. "We're researching three measly nickels, and instead of 15 cents, they're worth, let's see ..." He paused.

I started to reach for my notebook and pencil. But there was no need.

"Five hundred eighty-five bucks," Aaron said quickly.

"I can't wait to see Mr. Doyle's reaction tomorrow morning when we tell him about the profit from the popcorn sale," Dynamike said.

"I can't wait for Friday's student council meeting," I said, "when Jo and Allison find out how well we did with such an unoriginal and worn-out idea." I mimicked Allison's voice and fluttered my eyelashes.

My two buddies cracked up.

I biked home as fast as I could from the coin shop because it was my mom's birthday, and Dad was taking us out to dinner to celebrate. No take-out or fast food for us tonight. We were going to the Golden Lion, Mom's favorite place to eat.

I was so filled with my news about the three-legged buffalo nickel, I was ready to burst, but I'd promised myself to play it cool, wait until Mom or Dad asked about the coin, and then casually explain how rich our student council was about to become.

As it turned out, when I got home there wasn't time to talk anyway. Dad had made early reservations since it was a school night. I had to hurry up, shower, and dress in my best pants and shirt, the ones I usually saved for church. I plastered down my cowlick in back, but had the feeling that it sprang up again the moment I walked away from the mirror.

Because we were early, the restaurant wasn't crowded, and we were quickly seated at a quiet table. The waiter handed each of us a menu with a flourish. It didn't take me long to decide which steak I wanted, but my mom was slow. She considered all the options.

Finally we ordered, and within just a few minutes, hot rolls, butter, and our Caesar salads arrived.

"Well, what did you learn about your three-legged buffalo at the coin shop today?" Dad asked as we started our salads.

This was the moment I'd been waiting for. "You won't believe how much that nickel's worth," I blurted out, forgetting all about being cool and casual. And before either of them could even try to make a guess, I continued. "Mr. Jennings, the coin dealer here in town, says he'll sell that nickel for ..." Here I paused to give full dramatic effect and wished there was only a drum roll. "... $365."

"What!" My mom has perfect manners, but I think she almost dropped her salad fork. "Imagine someone paying that much money for a defective nickel." She shook her head in disbelief.

Dad laughed. "Defective nickel? I don't think that's quite the way numismatists look at it." Then he turned to me. "But it is a lot of money. If he thinks he can sell it for that, how much will Mr. Jennings pay you for it, Wink?"

"He was ready to hand over 250 bucks on the spot. But I told him I'd have to wait until I talk this over with Mr. Doyle tomorrow morning."

"I guess I don't understand about coins, but I do know that's wonderful news for your student council," Mom said. "What a great start to your term as treasurer. I'd call that one terrific popcorn sale!"

The food was great, so I didn't mind the white table-cloths or the waiters in their black ties and jackets who hovered and bobbed over us like magpies. Every time I took a sip of ice water, my glass magically filled again. Now that I'd shared my news, I could concentrate on my steak, and it was worth concentrating on. Between it and a gigantic baked potato, I stuffed myself.

That is, I thought I was stuffed, until one of the waiters came to our table and showed us the dessert tray. Choices, choices, choices. That's when I realized that I'd saved enough room for a big slice of the double deadly chocolate cake with chocolate icing.

As soon as we got back home, I ran upstairs to get the gift and spring my birthday surprise on Mom. I'd bought a card that wasn't too mushy, wrapped the present in blue paper, and put a white stick-on bow on top.

"Happy birthday!" I said, handing her the package.

"Thank you, Wink." Mom sat down with her present on her lap and started to read the card. She always does this, and I can't understand it. Everyone knows that first you tear open the package and check out the gift. Then, maybe, you look at the card. But Mom read every word. I was glad that I'd picked out one with a really short verse.

Finally she opened the box and uncovered the special coffee mug from the crumpled newspaper I'd stuffed around it. She set the mug on the coffee table in front of the couch. It looked like a fat, headless statue, standing on two big, bare feet. She and my dad both laughed.

"I love it, Wink."

"You lose your coffee cup a lot," I pointed out. "I thought maybe you could train this mug to come running when you whistle."

"I'll start training it tomorrow," she promised before reaching up to give me a big hug.

Birthday or not, I had to go upstairs then and do my homework. When I finally turned out the light and went to bed, I couldn't sleep for a while. Too much excitement packed into one day, I guess. I kept thinking about the nickel and wondering what Mr. Doyle would say.

>·+>·O·<+·+<

Sure enough, the next morning when I ran downstairs, Mom was drinking her coffee out of Big Feet. I knew when I first laid eyes on that mug that it was going to become her favorite companion, and it looked as if I was absolutely right. "You're up early," she said.

"Have to talk with Mr. Doyle before school about the popcorn sale," I reminded her. But I didn't try to leave without breakfast. Mom would never allow it. So I gobbled down some cereal and drank a glass of orange juice as fast as I could.

I hooked up with my buddies, and once again Dynamike, Aaron, and I hurried down the empty school halls to Mr. Doyle's room. He already had the cash box on his desk and had read through my report before we got there.

"Great job!" he said, all smiles. "The student council's not broke any more."

"Wait till you hear the whole story," Aaron said. He looked at me, and I began the tale.

Mr. Doyle had a pleased smile on his face when I started, but after I finished telling him about the three-legged buffalo nickel and how much it might be worth, his jaw flopped open. He was absolutely flabbergasted.

"You mean that one nickel is worth $250?"

"That's right," I assured him.

"I hardly know what to say." He ran his hands through his hair. "Of course, a valuable coin like that should be returned. Clearly it was spent by mistake. But how can we identify the owner? Hundreds of people bought popcorn at the fair. Obviously the person who spent the nickel didn't realize it was valuable. Let me think a minute," he said. He sat there for a moment, drumming his fingers on his desk.

While Mr. Doyle was thinking, I was worrying—big time! And the longer he thought, the more I worried. My heart was beating fast, keeping up with the drumming on the desk. It was beginning to look as if we weren't going to be able to sell the nickel after all.

"Tell you what I think we should do," Mr. Doyle finally said. "We should run an ad in the paper in the lost and found, and give the owner a chance to claim it. I'll donate the cost of the ad."

"But if we advertise that we've found a valuable three-legged buffalo nickel," I protested, "what's to keep just anybody from claiming it? It's not as if we've got fingerprints or anything."

"We'll be careful," Mr. Doyle explained. "I'll word the ad something like, 'If you're missing a valuable coin and can identify it in detail, call this number.' I won't use my name because that would connect me with the school. I'll just use initials. Then I'll give my home number. If anyone does call, I'll ask them what kind of a coin they lost and where they think they may have lost or spent it."

"Yeah," Aaron agreed. He gazed at Mr. Doyle in admiration. Clearly, he thought this plan was a worthy one. "I get it. With all the possible valuable coins it might be, only a person who really did realize he or she spent a three-legged buffalo nickel at the fair will be able to tell you about it."

"How long do we have to run the ad?" I asked, hoping we wouldn't be waiting around for weeks.

"It's a long shot that anyone who spent the coin will see it. But I feel we should try. Ads are expensive, but we should run it at least twice. I'll stop at the newspaper office after school and run the ad for two nights, Thursday and Friday, in the lost and found section. I'll feel a lot better if we make some attempt to try to find the owner. If we hear nothing by noon on Saturday, we'll consider the fact that a valuable coin ended up at our popcorn booth a lucky accident."

Then he grinned. "And if no one claims it, it'll be the only popcorn sale in the history of the school to make over a $300 profit!"

With permission to sell the coin on Saturday afternoon and have the check made out to Hennessey School Student Council, unless we got a response to our ad, I was walking on air. Mr. Doyle promised to keep the big news quiet until the student council meeting next week when I'd give my report.

Both Thursday and Friday night I read every word in the lost and found section of the newspaper. Our ad was there, in a box, big and bold. I clipped both ads out and put them in the WHAM Agency file folder that I kept in my desk drawer. I knew Mr. Doyle would call me right away if he had any news, and he didn't. I'd never phoned a teacher at home before, but using his number in the ad, I called and checked with him anyway late on Saturday morning, just to be sure. No one had answered the ad.

So on Saturday afternoon, Aaron, Dynamike, and I biked back to the coin shop with the nickel safely tucked in my pocket. We told Mr. Jennings about the ad and how we had tried without luck to locate the owner. Mr. Jennings wrote out a check on the spot. His eyes twinkled, and he seemed almost as pleased as we were.

I held the check in my hand looking carefully at both the words and the numbers. Sure enough—$250! I folded it neatly in half and placed it carefully in my shirt pocket.

"It's a pleasure to do business with you," he said, and shook hands with each of us.

On Monday, I gave the check to Mr. Doyle to deposit. Then I waited for the following Friday afternoon when the student council would meet. When the hour finally arrived for the meeting, I walked down the hall with Jo and Allison. We walked fast. Clearly Allison was bursting with importance and ready to spring her new plan. I tried hard not to give away that I, too, had big news to share.

We heard the minutes of the last meeting from the secretary. Allison read too fast in her high, squeaky voice, but I had to admit she hadn't missed anything that went on. Then Brett called on me to give the treasurer's report.

I cleared my throat and read loudly, "Cash on hand at our last meeting, $3.11. Cash on hand currently from profits on the popcorn sale and after paying all expenses and donating money to the Philharmonic Orchestra, $308.06."

As soon as I finished reading, I smiled straight at Allison. She had stopped writing in her notebook, and stared at me, pencil poised in the air. The look on her face had been worth waiting for. A combination of amazement and disbelief.

"How much was that again?" she asked.

"$308.06," I repeated. Those words were music to my ears.

A tremendous buzzing erupted from around the table. Brett finally broke in. "Wink," he said, looking uncomfortable and trying hard to be extra polite, "I know we did well at the popcorn sale. But are you sure you've got the numbers right? I was expecting maybe $50 profit."

"He's absolutely right," Mr. Doyle said. He wore a huge smile.

At that point, I spoke up. "You see, we didn't make all that money on popcorn; we made it by selling a valuable coin." Then I explained about the three-legged buffalo. It was hard to restore order, but finally Brett got us through Old Business and into New Business.

Although my news had taken some of the wind out of her sails, Allison launched right into her plans for holding an all-school carnival. Everybody seemed to think it would be a lot of fun. And I was feeling so good that even I supported it. Since everyone on student council currently regarded me as some sort of local hero, I had to act the part.

Of course after the student council members scattered, the news about our valuable nickel spread fast. For days after the council meeting, Aaron, Dynamike, and I were celebrities, particularly in the school cafeteria. Whether we were standing in line or sitting at the table eating our lunches, kids kept bringing coins up to us. Aaron brought his dad's new coin books to school so that we could look up anything that seemed really promising.

"How much is this dime worth?" some first grader would ask hopefully, plopping a dime down on the table that looked as if it had been run over by several trucks.

"Is this penny worth a million dollars?" another little kid would say, jumping up and down, and waving a coin in front of my face.

Even the school secretary stopped me one day. "Would you mind taking a quick look at this?" she asked. She took a coin wrapped in tissue out of her purse. I checked the date and mint in the coin book and found her quarter was worth exactly 25 cents. I returned it with regrets but was sure to hand her a WHAM Agency card.

Everybody in the school seemed to think that we were experts and that each coin in their pocket was worth a fortune. They never were.

In homeroom, we tried to decide what we wanted to do for a booth at the all-school carnival. One day during a discussion, someone suggested, "Since our class has such good artists, maybe we could sponsor a face-painting booth."

"Great idea!" Jo said. "I hope no other class thinks of it. I wonder if an art shop would donate the paints and brushes?"

Jo has always been a puzzlement to me. She's smart and friendly and nice. But I've never been able to understand her awful taste in friends. She and Allison stuck together like glue.

Everyone in the class agreed to the face-painting booth, so we formed committees. Aaron and I would take a turn on the ticket-taking committee, and Dynamike was one of the four kids selected to do the face painting. I found myself looking forward to the carnival, partly because I thought it would be fun and partly because it was bound to make more money for our treasury.

But I had another reason for anxiously awaiting the school carnival. The three-legged buffalo was still very much on my mind. Even though Mr. Doyle's ad was no longer running, and we'd sold the coin, I kept reading the lost and found section every night in the paper. There was never an ad offering a reward for a lost coin.

Had some little kid raided his father's or his mother's coin collection and used the valuable coins for spending money? And once his parents found out, if the little kid told them he'd spent money at our popcorn sale, would they come to school and ask about it? What would we do? The coin might be sold by then and couldn't be returned. Would we need to take the money out of our treasury?

All I could do was worry. Without any leads, the WHAM Agency had nothing to go on. Where had that three-legged buffalo come from? As far as I could see, there were only two ways to find out. Either someone appeared and explained how the coin had been accidentally spent, or another coin turned up giving us more clues. That was a long shot, but the WHAM Agency was alert and on the job. Right after the school carnival we'd check every coin that was taken in that night.

6

Friday night was cold and clear. Parking spaces, scarce at best, were non-existent on special nights like concerts and carnivals. Street parking was almost as bad, so Mom, Dad, and I decided to walk. We left in plenty of time to get to the carnival early, but apparently, so did everyone else.

When we arrived, there was a huge crowd in the front hall of the school, and the gym doors hadn't even opened yet. It sure looked like the carnival would be a big success. I knew I'd have to put up with Allison being smug about that, but I could handle it. As student council treasurer, I couldn't help but hope for a big haul even if it was her idea.

Once inside the school, we got in a line, and Dad bought strips of tickets at the ticket booth. Mr. Doyle was there helping out. Brett and Cindy were taking in money and handing out tickets as fast as they could.

As I looked over the counter at the quickly-filling cash box, I felt a little tingle knowing that soon Aaron, Dynamike, and I would be carefully examining every one of those coins. Even though I told myself lightning doesn't strike twice, my heart still beat a little faster as

I thought about it. I automatically felt for the cash box key that I always wore now on a chain around my neck. It was there, safely tucked under my T-shirt.

We found a spot to stand, past the drinking fountains and away from the ticket sellers. Smushed almost flat against the wall, I caught sight of a white-haired man in a blue beret and a way-too-big suit fighting his way through the crowd. For some reason, he looked vaguely familiar to me. Where had I seen him before?

Dad tore off a few tickets from the strip that he bought and put them in his pocket. He gave most of the strip to me.

"I'm working at my class face-painting booth with Aaron taking tickets from seven to seven-thirty," I explained, looking at my watch. "So I've got to hurry."

"Okay," Dad said. "Go have fun, and let's meet here by the fountains at nine o'clock."

As I threaded my way through the crowd, I tried to catch another glimpse of the man in the blue beret, but I didn't see him. "I'm working the first shift," I explained to the girl guarding the gym door. She let me in.

Brett Wallace had turned out to be a great student council president. He gave everyone something to do, and once he did, he stopped worrying about it. He trusted people to carry out their assignments. That gave him time to concentrate on what he called "the big picture." Yesterday he gave maps he'd made of the gym and cafeteria to each class showing them where to set up the booths.

As I looked around, I thought, if there was chaos inside the gym, at least it was organized chaos. I headed for the west wall, where I spied Dynamike and Theresa Martinez. They were our class artists assigned for the first hour.

When I reached them, I said, "Awesome!"

They were both wearing bright red artist paint smocks with flowing puffy sleeves provided by Theresa's mother, who was always sewing costumes for one occasion or another. They had already painted each other's faces. Dynamike had a rainbow on the left side of his face, and a big black thundercloud with lightning and rain drops on the right side. Theresa looked like a cross between a Valentine and a Frankenstein. One side was hearts and flowers. The other side had scars and stitches.

Aaron was already sitting behind a small table in front of the booth ready to take tickets. I quickly dropped into the seat next to him. Customers could enter our booth on either Dynamike's or Theresa's side. There were two stools for the subjects, and two hand mirrors so that customers could take a look at the finished painting.

"We've decided to charge one ticket for each side of the face," Dynamike explained.

"Good idea," I agreed.

"And we've been practicing, so we're really fast," Theresa said. "No one will stand around long waiting."

Once the gym doors opened, there was a crush of customers. And Theresa was wrong. A line formed immediately at our booth. We were glad to have so many early customers, because they'd be walking advertisements. Ours was going to be one of the most popular spots at the carnival.

One of the first to come to have her face painted was Allison, followed by her little sister, Mary Margaret. I managed not to groan audibly.

"Just one side for me," Allison said, handing over a ticket to Aaron and heading toward Theresa's side of the booth. "I'd like some hearts and flowers."

"I want to be a tiger," Mary Margaret demanded.

"That'll be two tickets," I said.

"Two! How come?"

"It costs one ticket for each side of the face," I explained, pointing to the little sign Aaron had pinned up. "Do you want to be a tiger on only one side or on both sides?"

Mary Margaret scowled, but handed over two crumpled tickets and climbed up on a stool in front of Dynamike. I pitied him.

The artists set to work. Allison was soon looking in the mirror and admiring a tiny red heart, surrounded by a sprinkling of white daisies with a blue ribbon circling it. She stepped out of the way to wait for Mary Margaret and to let in the next customer.

Finally Dynamike finished. "There you are," he said and handed Mary Margaret the mirror.

She frowned. "I look like a silly old pussycat, not a tiger."

Dynamike had painted whiskers and some great cat eyes. He seemed disappointed when Mary Margaret complained, but he aimed to please. "Would you like me to add some fangs, like a saber-toothed tiger?" he asked.

The frown vanished. "Yes!"

A couple of minutes later, a fierce, saber-toothed tiger left the booth, smiling broadly.

When our half-hour was up and our replacements came, Aaron and I left Theresa and Dynamike to finish their shift, and we started through the carnival. There was such a crush of people that you had to be pretty determined to get anywhere.

Right next to us, the first graders had their lollipop tree. You paid a ticket, stepped up, and pulled a lollipop off a cardboard tree. You could only see the top of the lollipop when you picked it, but some of the lollipops had colored tape wrapped around their sticks, and if you picked one of these, you got a prize.

Aaron picked a red lollipop.

"Hey! Look!" I yelled, when I picked a green one and found yellow tape on the stick. "I get a prize!" A first grader handed me a yellow pencil, which I stuck in my pocket. I grinned. It wasn't often I beat Aaron at anything, even picking lollipops!

The next booth was run by a group of fifth graders. The big sign painted in bright blue letters above the booth read, "Flags of the World." The back wall of the booth was covered in brightly colored, miniature flags.

Each flag was taped up with a number above it. You reached in a glass bowl and pulled out a slip of paper with a number on it. Then you looked for the flag with a matching number. If you could tell which country's flag it was, you won a prize.

I paid my ticket and drew number 27. I looked at the corresponding flag and was puzzled. It reminded me a lot of the American flag. There were red and white stripes but only one star up in the corner. I groaned. I had no idea which country the flag was from. I looked hopefully at Aaron, who smiled but didn't say a word. I knew that he knew which country's flag it was. I looked at the lone star again. "Texas?" I said.

Aaron laughed. "Texas is big, Wink. But it's not a country."

"That's the flag of the Republic of Liberia," the fifth grader running the booth informed me after looking it up on his answer sheet. Then he took Aaron's ticket. Aaron reached in the bowl and pulled out number 41.

I noticed that this flag was red, white, and blue, too. There were red and white stripes in the corner and four red stars on a blue field. Again, I had no idea. I shook my head. "New Zealand," Aaron promptly said.

"That's right!" The fifth grader handed over a prize. It was a ballpoint pen.

I didn't feel so bad when I saw the prize. I'd rather have a pencil than a pen any day. It makes it a lot easier to crase mistakes.

As we turned to leave, I caught sight of the man in the blue beret again. I guess he stood out because he wasn't wearing casual clothes like everyone else. His dark suit seemed about two sizes too big for him. The pants hung down and touched the floor. His head was turned, but I could see he had a lot of white hair tucked under a blue beret. I watched him pull out an old-fashioned coin purse, and then I heard one of the women who was helping in the first grade booth explain that none of the booths took money, and he'd need to buy a strip of tickets from the cashier in the hall.

My antennae were up. In fact, they were wiggling. Why did this guy look kind of familiar to me? Had I seen him at the popcorn sale? I decided to follow him. Familiar or not, this guy struck me as the kind of old man who might have a purse filled with valuable coins.

"Hey! What's happening over there?" Aaron said.

I turned my head to look where Aaron was pointing.

There was a lot of laughing and yelling going on in the far corner.

"Come on," Aaron said, and took off.

I turned back to look for the old man in the beret, but he'd disappeared into the mass of people. Which direction had he gone? I was mad at myself for losing sight of him, but since Aaron was already working his way toward the corner, I turned and hurried after him.

Mr. Doyle's fifth graders had made an old western-style cardboard jail. It had two large windows, each with thick black bars. There was a big sign above it.

Christmas lights pushed through holes of the sign blinked on and off and spelled out: "The Calaboose." In front, several kids were dressed as cowboys and cowgirls. They had tossed a rope around someone and were leading her off to jail.

"Look!" I said, when I got close enough to see what was happening. "They're locking up Mrs. Tilden!"

Two of the fifth graders led her through a cardboard door into the jail, where she peered out from behind the cardboard bars. Mrs. Tilden was laughing as she looked out at the crowd that had gathered.

A fifth grader, parading in front, wearing a sheriff's star, cowboy hat, vest, and boots with silver spurs, announced loudly, "Will somebody take pity on a lady in distress? She got locked up for speeding past our booth. This poor miserable prisoner needs two tickets to pay her fine. She's stuck in this here jail until the fine is paid in full."

"Here's our chance to be heroes and save our teacher," I whispered to Aaron. He nodded.

"We'll pay the fine," I yelled, tearing off a ticket. Aaron handed over another one.

"All right!" the fifth grader said, releasing Mrs. Tilden. "You're lucky that these young cowpokes came to your rescue, ma'am. Now you'd better keep out of trouble for the rest of the evening."

"Oh, I will," Mrs. Tilden promised. "Thank you, boys," she said to us. "I'd hate to have spent the whole evening locked up in there!" She hurried off and seemed to be glad to put some distance between herself and the Calaboose.

As we continued to watch, two of the fifth grade deputies grabbed Mr. Tobias, our principal, and pulled him into the jail. But Aaron and I walked on, leaving him to be bailed out by someone else.

"I want to check on something," I said, and moving as fast as I could through the crowd, I led the way into the hall to the cashier's booth.

"What's up?" Aaron asked when he caught up with me.

"Just a hunch," I said.

Brett and Cindy were still on duty. Most of the crowd seemed to be inside already, but people kept drifting in. There were two short lines, and I joined the one leading to Brett. When I made my way to the front, I asked, "Did an old guy with white hair wearing a blue beret stop here a few minutes ago to buy tickets?"

"Yeah," Brett said. "Why?"

"Did he pay for the tickets with paper money or with coins?" I persisted.

Suddenly a look of understanding passed across Brett's face. "You think that maybe ..." Brett lowered his voice. "Let me think. Yeah, I remember. He paid in coins. Just bought a dollar's worth, I think. And he counted them out one by one from an old coin purse."

A woman behind us spoke up then, "I'd like to buy some tickets, boys. Could you visit later?"

Reluctantly I stepped out of line. I was just dying to get my hands on that cash box, but I realized I couldn't do it right then. As we headed back into the gym, I described the old man to Aaron. "Do you remember anyone like that from the popcorn sale?" I asked.

"No," Aaron said. "You've got three-legged buffalo on the brain."

I wasn't going to give up easily. "Let's split up and see if we can spot him and find out who he is," I said. "Then we'll meet back here."

Aaron headed off in one direction, and I went in the other. I kept looking for a blue beret above the shoulders of the crowd. It was probably the only hat in the gym and shouldn't be that hard to spot ... But I didn't see it.

Ten minutes later, we connected again. "No sign of him," Aaron said. "How about you?"

I shrugged.

We saw a ball toss that we wanted to try. For a ticket, you got three softballs that you threw under-handed into an old fashioned milk can with a narrow neck. We watched Mrs. Carabell and her friend try pitching unsuccessfully before our turn.

"Hello there, Wink!" Mrs. Carabell said. "This is my friend, Doris McCorkle. Doris, this is Wink and Aaron. They have a tree house on my vacant lot. They're two of the private investigators I told you about who found my missing cat."

I smiled and couldn't help wishing that I could add the Case of the Three-Legged Buffalo to the list of mysteries I'd solved.

"Hello," Mrs. McCorkle said. "I hope you boys have better aim than we did. We'll watch and cheer you on."

"I'll give it a try," I said. I aimed, threw, and missed twice. "Darn!" My third ball rolled around the rim and then fell off.

"Too bad," Mrs. McCorkle sympathized. "You were close."

Aaron tried next, and his very first ball went in. The second one barely missed. And his third ball dropped in, too. Mrs. Carabell and Mrs. McCorkle clapped enthusiastically.

"Two balls in the milk can," the fourth grader yelled. "Two prizes." Aaron was handed two tiny potted ivy plants, and suddenly I was glad I hadn't won. The last thing I wanted was to carry around plants all night. But, as usual, Aaron thought fast.

"The prizes go to my cheering section," Aaron said, handing one plant to Mrs. Carabell and another to Mrs. McCorkle.

"Why, thank you!" each of the ladies cried.

"You're welcome," Aaron said.

"Let's head for the cafeteria," I told Aaron. "We need to check out the food. You know Dynamike will want a full report for when he gets off duty. He'll be hungry. Besides, that's the one place we haven't looked yet for the old man in the blue beret."

Once Aaron and I jostled our way through the noisy, happy crowd and into the cafeteria, we were almost knocked over by a wonderful buttery smell. Maybe because they'd heard about the big money student council had made last month, or maybe because they liked to eat it as much as I do, the second graders had decided to sell popcorn. And if anything smells better than freshly popped hot popcorn, I don't know what it is.

"I want a bag," I said. I didn't care whether or not the idea was as unoriginal as Allison Parsley thought. It smelled good to me. And apparently Aaron agreed, because he quickly handed over a ticket to get his own bag.

As we enjoyed our snack, we circled the cafeteria, looking for the man in the blue beret. I thought I spied him once, through a brief break in the sea of people, over by the far wall. In my haste to reach him, I'm afraid I bumped quite a few people. But when I finally managed to reach the spot, he was gone. The room was packed, so it wasn't going to be easy to find anyone.

"Let's split up," I finally said to Aaron. "Cruise around in a circle and see if you can find any sign of the old guy."

"Okay," Aaron agreed.

But then I hesitated for a moment. "What'll we do if we find him?"

"Strike up a conversation," Aaron advised. "You're part of the WHAM Agency. Be an investigator. Find out who he is and what brings him to the school tonight. You know, casual like. Pump him for information."

"Right," I agreed. I took off in one direction, and Aaron started in the other.

The kindergartners were running a bake sale called Tempting Treats. From what I'd seen of kindergartners' hands, plus what I knew about the toads, beetles, frogs, fish, and the rat that lived in the science lab where the ovens they used were located, I wasn't even slightly tempted. No one in his right mind would be willing to risk eating cookies that kindergartners had baked in the science room.

But in addition to the tray of fresh-baked classroom cookies, the parents of kindergartners had helped out by making brownies and cakes at home and bringing them to the sale. These looked fantastic, and I was sure their booth would be a big money maker.

I spied my folks not far away. "Hey! Mom! Dad!" I yelled.

They saw me and worked their way over. Mom was carrying a paper plate piled high with brownies and Dad was carrying a chocolate cake, holding it up high to protect it from the throng.

"Wow!" I said, eyeing their purchases and happy that classroom cookies were not among them. "Looks good!"

"You know how I am about chocolate," Dad confessed. "I had to go back to the front hall and buy more tickets."

"We were just talking with Aaron's folks a few minutes ago," Mom said, looking about. "Where's Aaron?"

"He's here somewhere," I said, not wanting to go into a long explanation about how we had split up to search for an old man in a blue beret.

"It's a great carnival," Mom said, "but I'm tired and almost ready to head for home. Aaron's parents told us they'd give you a ride, Wink."

"That'll save me a trip back," Dad said. "You know we don't want you out walking alone at night, and especially not tonight when you're carrying money."

Aaron joined us just in time to hear my dad's last comment. "Hi, Mr. and Mrs. Winklehockey. Sure, we'll give him a ride home. We're taking Dynamike, too."

"And I won't have too much money to carry," I said. "Mr. Doyle and Brett will keep and count all the checks and paper money from tonight, and then Mr. Doyle will lock it away for safekeeping. My only job is to take home the cash box and tally up all the change." I didn't add that there could be a valuable coin somewhere among that change.

My folks started for the door, and Aaron and I continued circling the cafeteria.

"Any sign of the old guy?" I asked Aaron as soon as they were out of earshot.

"No," he said. "I wonder where he could have disappeared to? Of course, he could have gone home."

I grabbed Aaron's arm. "Look!" I said. "Over by the Tempting Treats banner. There he is with a plate of brownies. He's talking with Mrs. Carabell. Let's go get introduced."

We did everything but knock people over, and we earned a few dirty looks as we tried to shove our way through, but the seam in the crowd closed quickly and there was no way to move fast. By the time we made it across the room to Mrs. Carabell and Doris McCorkle, the old man in the beret was already shuffling toward the door. And Mrs. Carabell was busy talking to one of my least favorite people, the sour-faced cafeteria supervisor, Mrs. Wheaton. I always thought Mrs. Wheaton had about as much affection for kids as she did for ants.

"He's getting away," Aaron moaned. "What'll we do?"

"Darn!" I said. "We can't very well chase after him and demand to look in his coin purse. And with old lady Wheaton there, I don't want to try to bust in and talk to Mrs. Carabell right now."

I looked at my watch and let out a sigh of exasperation. We'd had a perfectly good clue and lost it. "There's nothing we can do about it tonight anyway. When we count the money tomorrow, if there are any interesting coins, I'll call Mrs. Carabell and get the scoop on the old guy. She was talking with him, so she must know who he is."

"Right." Aaron brightened a little, although I could tell he was as frustrated as I was. "He doesn't look at all familiar to me," Aaron confessed, "and I don't really think we're going to find any more valuable nickels. But I have to admit, he does look like the type of eccentric old guy who might be carrying around rare coins."

We stood there for a moment, and then I said, "It's almost time for Dynamike to get off duty. Come on. Maybe there'll be time for him to paint our faces."

The line at our class booth was short, so Aaron and I joined it for a face painting job by Dynamike.

"I'm tired of painting the same old thing," Dynamike said. "Scars and stitches. How about if I turn you two into Greek monsters?"

"Sure," we agreed.

"Argus had a hundred eyes," Dynamike told Aaron as he set to work painting eyes all over Aaron's face. He soon looked fantastic. Just as I climbed up on the stool for my turn, Dynamike's replacement arrived.

"Hey, I'll stay a few minutes longer to take care of Wink," Dynamike volunteered. He worked fast, and in almost no time Dynamike said, "Done."

I looked in the mirror and grinned. Instead of eyes painted all over my face, I had just one huge bloodshot eye painted in the center of my forehead. I looked truly scary. "What am I?" I asked.

"Cyclops," Dynamike answered, "You remember, the one-eyed Greek monster?"

I didn't remember, but I was happy with the effect. I had never paid much attention in class when we studied the Greeks. I thought it was all temples and old marble statues that were missing arms. If they had monsters like Argus and Cyclops, maybe I'd have given the Greeks another chance.

Dynamike quickly unsnapped his artist smock and turned it over to Miguel.

It didn't surprise me at all when Dynamike said, "Let's go to the cafeteria." That kid is always hungry.

On the way there, Aaron and I described to Dynamike our suspicions about the old guy in the beret.

"Wow," Dynamike said. "I wish I could have seen him."

"Do you remember anyone like that from the popcorn sale?" I asked.

Dynamike shook his head.

We took a detour to see Brett at the ticket booth. There were only a few people there, just those who were coming to buy more strips of tickets.

"Hi, Wink," Brett called. "As soon as you left, I tried to take a look at some of the coins, but it was hopeless. Money was coming in and going out so fast, that old guy could have given me a valuable coin and I might have handed it over in change to the next customer."

My heart sank. I hadn't thought of that. What if Brett had actually let a valuable coin slip right through his fingers? More than ever, I wanted to get my hands on that money. "I'll be back at nine-thirty to pick up the cash box," I said.

We continued on to the cafeteria, where Dynamike got some popcorn before going to the Tempting Treats booth. "Look at that great cake!" he said, pointing to one that had little marshmallows and pieces of nuts sticking out of the thick chocolate icing. "That's for me!"

Dynamike had bought 20 tickets for five dollars, and so far had spent only one of them on popcorn. Now he peeled off 16 of his tickets for the cake of his dreams.

"It looks delicious," Aaron agreed, "but now you're stuck with carrying it everywhere we go. Do you think you could leave it here with your name on it and pick it up when it's time to leave?"

"No way," Dynamike said. "These kids may be kindergartners, but they're smart. They'd sell it again."

We walked back through the gym. I held Dynamike's cake while he tried tossing bean bags through the open mouth of a wooden clown that the fourth graders had made.

"How do you like that!" he asked, after putting all three bags through the mouth.

"Way to go," Aaron said. "No doubt about it. You're a champion at putting things into mouths."

"Here's your prize," a fourth grader said, handing over a fluorescent orange yo-yo, which Dynamike stuffed in his pocket. I handed back his cake.

By nine-thirty, we had no more tickets, and the crowd in the gym was thinning out. I went back to the ticket booth. Mr. Doyle had taken out all the paper money, so I took the cash box from Brett and locked it, and then hung the key back around my neck. While I was doing that, Aaron and Dynamike went off to find Mr. and Mrs. Bates.

There was a crush in the hall as people headed toward the exit. I edged toward the inside wall and bent to tie a shoelace. Suddenly, I heard a loud "Grrrr!" Startled, I felt something pounce on my back. "Grrrr!" I heard again, while someone's arm went in front of my throat and legs wound around my waist. Then another hand attacked and pulled at my hair.

"Get off of me!" I yelled, standing up straight and try-ing to turn my head enough to scare someone off with my Cyclops eye, while defending myself with one arm and hanging tightly onto the cash box with the other.

"Mary Margaret!" I heard Allison shriek from behind me. "You get off of him."

"I'm not Mary Margaret," came the voice from behind my neck. "I'm a ferocious saber-toothed tiger and this is my dinner!"

"Well, I'm a Cyclops and I eat little girls for late night snacks," I whispered fiercely.

She ignored me.

Allison and I tried to pull her off, but Mary Margaret just held on tighter. My neck was beginning to hurt. I was mad and embarrassed at the same time.

Suddenly Allison changed her approach. Using a wheedling voice she asked, "Isn't it time for the saber-toothed tiger to have dessert?" She held out one of the brownies that she had bought at the Tempting Treats booth.

"Grrrr!" Mary Margaret replied. But she loosened her grip, slid down my back, and reached out for her treat. Then the two of them pushed away through the crowd without even a backward look or a "sorry."

As I started looking for my friends again, I reached up and felt the scratches on my face and neck. She hadn't actually taken a bite out of me, but I did have scars from my battle with the beast. My only consolation was that it probably made my Cyclops appearance even more frightening.

"What happened to you?" Dynamike asked staring at my hair and neck when he, Aaron, and Aaron's parents finally reached me.

"It's partly your fault," I grumbled. "You put such a realistic face on Mary Margaret that she turned into an attacking saber-tooth! I was her unfortunate victim."

Mr. Bates led the way to the parking lot and we all climbed into the car, with Dynamike carefully balancing his cake as he settled into his place.

"It looked like a very successful carnival," Mrs. Bates commented from the front seat. "I wonder how much money you made?"

"The tickets were in rolls of a thousand," I explained. "And Brett said they were on their fourth roll of tickets when the carnival ended."

"So they took in between $750 and $1,000," Aaron, the brain, calculated quickly. "Wow!"

"And there were hardly any expenses," I added. "Norm, the custodian, is even donating his overtime to help with the cleanup."

I sat there dying to open the cash box held tightly on my lap. Did it hold a coin that would add even more to the profits? "Do you think there's enough light from the street lamps to check out the coins as we drive?" I asked.

"Wink, you know you're going to need good light and maybe a magnifying glass," Mr. Bates reminded me.

"Could we go inside with Wink and check them out, just for a little bit?" Aaron pleaded.

"No," Mrs. Bates said. "I'm sorry, but if you do have a valuable coin, it will be there in the morning. It's almost ten o'clock. Wink's mother was tired and has probably gone to bed by now. We can't go barging in at this time of night."

The three of us in the back seat looked at each other and let out a collective sigh.

Once I was home, I said good-night to Dad who had waited up for me. Mrs. Bates was right. Mom was already asleep.

First I went into the bathroom and used a lot of soap and water to remove my Cyclops eye. I brushed my teeth and then headed off to my room, carrying the cash box with me and thinking about the fun we'd have at ten o'clock tomorrow morning when Dynamike and Aaron came to help me count the change. I was about to hide the box under my bed for safekeeping, when I stopped.

Why not scramble into my pj's fast and then take a quick peek in the cash box? My buddies would never know. And I promised myself I wouldn't make a thorough search tonight—just ten minutes, max, a sort of sneak preview of those piles and piles of coins we'd check tomorrow. I felt my heart begin to beat faster. Would there be another three-legged buffalo?

I set the cash box on my bed while I grabbed my pajamas out of the drawer. It was when I was pulling off my T-shirt that I first noticed. The chain that I'd been wearing around my neck all night with the key to the cash box on it was missing! I clutched at my neck and stood there frozen, hit by a feeling of panic.

It's hard to describe the feeling in your stomach when you first realize you've lost something important. It's like the lurch of an elevator or the sensation of a glass slipping through your fingers. Quick, sick, and awful. I tried not to panic even as I kept groping around my neck for something that I now knew wasn't there. After all, I thought, it's only a key. I hadn't lost the cash box or the student council's money.

But talking calmly to myself didn't help. I wanted to look in the cash box right now. I'd been wanting to search through those coins all night long. First I lost the old guy in the blue beret, and now the key. And I was embarrassed, too. That key was important. It was a symbol of my office, and I had worn it proudly.

I plopped myself down on the edge of the bed and ran my fingers through my hair as I groaned aloud. How could anyone trust a treasurer who couldn't even keep track of the key to the cash box?

Even though I knew the key was gone, I forced myself to check my room carefully just to make sure that I hadn't accidentally pulled off the key and chain with my shirt. I checked every inch of the bedspread. Then I got down on my hands and knees to feel around under the bed and on the floor.

I was desperate. That key had to be here, and of course, it wasn't. It wasn't on the bed or the floor.

I ran downstairs not bothering to stop to pull my pajama top on.

"Wink! What are you doing up still?" Dad asked when I came charging into the kitchen. He was drinking a cup of tea and studying a magazine article on woodworking. I knew he had borrowed some issues of a magazine that our library didn't carry so that he could get some help with his current project of building a storage cabinet and shelves in our garage.

"I've lost the key to the cash box," I blurted out, considerably louder than I'd intended. "I need to call Aaron and ask him to check and see if it might have fallen off in his dad's car on the way home."

Dad looked at the clock. "It's too late to call. I'm afraid you'll have to wait until morning."

I must have looked like I was going to cry, because Dad stood and patted my shoulder. "I know you're worried," he said. "But if the key's in Aaron's car, it will still be there in the morning. If not, we will have bothered his family for nothing."

I stared at the floor and nodded. He was right, of course.

"When do you last remember having it?" Dad asked.

"Right at nine-thirty when I went to the ticket table in the hall, I took the key off my neck and locked up the cash box. So I know I had it then." My voice rose again in a wail, and Dad gave me a warning shush with his finger. He didn't want me to wake up Mom.

"At the end of the carnival, there was a real crush in the hall. Everyone headed for the front doors at once," I continued, speaking more softly. "When I saw Dynamike, Aaron, and his folks, I ran up to them, and we went right out to the parking lot. We drove straight home, and I was the first one they dropped off."

"Hmmm," Dad said. "I suppose the key could have slipped off your neck in the parking lot. You can go over there first thing in the morning and look around when it's light. Or maybe it slipped off while you were in the front hall. The custodian may find it when he's sweeping up. If so, he's sure to put it in the lost and found."

The front hall! Of course! It was like a light bulb going off. That's when it must have happened. When Mary Margaret jumped on my back!

"Wink!" Dad said. He had finally taken a good look at me standing there wearing just my jeans. "Your face and neck are all scratched." He came closer for a better look, lifting up my chin and turning me toward the light. "Have you been in a fight?"

"Sort of," I admitted. "I was attacked by a saber-toothed tiger." Then, seeing the expression on his face, and realizing this was not the time for smart comments or riddles, I said, "Mary Margaret got her faced painted like a saber-toothed tiger, and she took on her role too seriously. When I wasn't expecting it, she jumped on my back and wouldn't let go. She almost strangled me. I think maybe that's when the key chain broke."

"I guess that could have happened," Dad agreed, as he sat again. "If she pulled on it while she was climbing up or down from your back, the chain may have come open or broken and the key might have fallen off right there in the hall."

"Or," I worried aloud, "Mary Margaret may have grabbed the key and chain when it broke open and taken them away with her as trophies when she went off to devour her brownie."

"Surely she wouldn't do that," Dad protested.

"You don't know Mary Margaret as well as I do." I balled my fists and felt my face getting hot. "Now that I think about it, I'm absolutely certain that Mary Margaret has my key. I'd like to go over there right now and find out."

"Well, you're not," Dad said. "It's too late for private investigating tonight. Tomorrow's time enough to check out Mary Margaret, the parking lot, and the Bates's car. If those are all dead ends, we'll have to wait until Monday and hope that the custodian found it. In the worst case, we'll get a new key made at the lock shop."

Wait until Monday! Those words echoed in my head. I wouldn't be able to stand it. I'd use a hammer and chisel and break into the box rather than wait all week-end to check out those coins. But how would I explain a broken cash box to Mr. Doyle and the student council? I didn't even want to admit to Aaron and Dynamike that I had lost the key, and they were my best buddies.

I was feeling miserable when I climbed back up the stairs and went to bed. But I didn't toss and turn as much as I thought I might. I think that was because I really wasn't worrying and wondering where the key might be. I was absolutely one-hundred-percent-positive-certain it was with Mary Margaret.

Even though I was up early the next morning, Dad was already out in the garage taking measurements to buy lumber for his new project. But he'd filled Mom in about my lost key.

"So where are you going to search for it?" she asked as I gulped down a quick breakfast.

"I'm not going to go over and search the parking lot at school. And I'm not going to call up the Bateses and ask them to check out the back seat of their car, either." I felt myself getting hot again. Even the thought of admitting to Aaron that I'd been robbed by Mary Margaret was humiliating.

"I know where that key is. I'm absolutely certain of it, and I'm going over to Mary Margaret's to demand it back. I won't leave until she hands it over."

"Hmmm. Do you think you have the right attitude for a job as delicate as this?" Mom asked, and paused as she sipped her coffee. "After all, Mary Margaret is very young. You can't simply accuse her and demand your key. For one thing, you don't know for sure that she has it. And, even if she does, there's no guarantee that if you act mean and nasty to her she'll be nice and willing to give it back."

"You've got that right," I admitted. "What I need is a plan." I thought hard. Unless I approached Mary Margaret with care, I might never see my key again. She might bury it in a hole in her backyard just for the fun of it. And even though I knew we could get a replacement key, it wouldn't be the same.

I looked at the clock. I had to act fast. Aaron and Dynamike would be coming over in about an hour. I couldn't face them without the key. I just couldn't.

"Take a minute to think about it," Mom continued. "From what you've told me, a mission involving Mary Margaret is not to be taken lightly."

An idea popped into my head. "A reward! Maybe I need to offer Mary Margaret a reward of some kind."

"Good thinking," Mom said. "Only this week, I read an article in one of my parenting magazines about avoiding tears and tantrums. It stressed the truth of an old saying: 'You catch more flies with honey than with vinegar'."

I thought about that for a moment. "Yeah," I agreed. "But what do I have for a reward that would be of any interest to Mary Margaret? I'm not giving her any money, that's for sure. And she isn't exactly into trading baseball cards." I thought some more. "Jewelry! Mom, do you have any old junk jewelry you could part with? You know, some girlie thing that's absolutely worthless?"

Suddenly Mom's face lit up, and she put down her coffee cup. "Come with me. I may have exactly what you need, Wink."

I followed Mom to her walk-in bedroom closet. She kept a pile of junk jewelry in a drawer in a wooden chest in there. Mom started to dig through the tangle of chains and bracelets and pins.

"Aha! Here it is," she said. "I knew I hadn't thrown it away." She took a small gold and black brocaded box out of the heap and opened it. Inside was a silver chain bracelet with a tiny heart and a key dangling from it.

I stared at my mother in astonishment. "You mean you think I should give this perfectly nice looking bracelet to Mary Margaret in exchange for my key?" I sputtered. "Isn't that bribery?"

"You know, I can see how you might look at it that way," Mom admitted. "But I think if I were you, and I wanted to get my key back, I'd just call it a reward for finding and returning your property." Mom smiled. "Think of it as sort of a fall-back Plan B, in case you don't get anywhere by just asking her to hand your key over."

I stood there doubtfully. This bracelet was too good for Mary Margaret. When I asked my mom about junk jewelry, I meant junk.

"Now if we knew for sure," Mom went on, "that Mary Margaret had deliberately taken your chain and key, we might approach this problem differently. But you really don't know that. It would be awful to accuse her of something she didn't do. Very embarrassing."

"But, Mom," I protested. "I'm sure she's got it."

"Absolutely positive?"

I squirmed just a little. "Almost absolutely positive."

"Right," Mom agreed. "Almost. That's why I think offering a little reward might be the best policy. If Plan A, asking for the key and chain outright, doesn't work, you'll have Plan B to fall back on."

"Maybe you're right," I admitted. After all, Mom knew a lot more about handling kids than I did. And she was definitely right about one thing. I couldn't afford to be wrong. If it should turn out that I accused her and had made a mistake about Mary Margaret, Allison would never let me forget it.

I put the bracelet back inside and slipped the little box into my pocket. "Thanks, Mom. I'll go over there right now."

"And remember," she said. "Be pleasant. Use tact and diplomacy."

When I rang the bell at the Parsleys, Allison came to the door. "What do you want?" she asked. So much for pleasantries.

"I'd like to speak with Mary Margaret, please," I explained, managing a polite smile as I stood on the doorstep.

Allison's eyes widened. "Come on in." She led me into the family room where Mary Margaret was sitting on the floor in front of the TV. She was wearing jeans and a T-shirt, and I was pretty sure I caught the glint of a chain showing around the back of her neck. She hadn't washed her face. The whiskers, cat's eyes, and fangs were still there.

"Wink wants to talk with you," Allison said. Then, not even trying to be casual about it, she sat down on the edge of the couch and leaned forward to listen, clearly intrigued about what I wanted with her sister.

I took a deep breath and kept smiling. "Mary Margaret, I think you may have something of mine."

Mary Margaret glared at me. She didn't say a word but suddenly clutched at something beneath the front of her T-shirt. I was positive I knew what the object was.

"I lost something important at the carnival last night, and I think you may have found it. Will you give it back to me?" I went on.

Mary Margaret continued staring, shut her jaw tight, and vigorously shook her head no. Suddenly, she stuck her tongue out at me, then turned her back, and started watching TV again.

So much for Plan A.

I was glad that, thanks to Mom, I was ready with Plan B. I resisted the urge to run over and throttle Mary Margaret. Instead, I turned, sighed loudly, and took a couple steps toward the door.

"That's really too bad," I said, speaking loudly enough so that Mary Margaret could hear while pretending to be explaining all this to Allison. "You see, I'm offering a very valuable reward to the person who finds and returns to me what I lost." I reached in my pocket and held out the brocaded box.

Out of the corner of my eye, I watched Mary Margaret turn her head, stare, and hesitate. I held my breath. If this didn't work, I wasn't sure what I'd do next. I didn't have a Plan C. Mary Margaret put me out of my misery by taking the bait.

She scrambled up off the carpet. "Is this what you lost?" she asked innocently, pulling my key on the chain out from under her T-shirt and holding it out to show it to me.

"That's it," I said. I felt a surge of triumph. She reached out for the box.

"Ah, ah, ah," I said, holding the box high. "Hand over the key chain first."

She took a step toward me. I held out my empty hand for the chain and key, while I lowered my other hand and held out the little jewel box, almost like a carrot, in front of her nose.

Mary Margaret hesitated again before she finally pulled off the chain with the key from around her neck and handed it to me, at the same time grabbing the box. I didn't stick around to wait and see her open it.

Quickly I slipped the chain over my head and tucked the key under my shirt. Breathing a big sigh of relief, I continued on out the door. Plan B had worked.

"Mom!" I heard Allison shriek as she ran into the kitchen. "Wait till you find out what Mary Margaret did. I think she should be punished."

I smiled. Allison's tattling was finally good for something!

As I jogged home, I joyfully felt each little jangle of the key on the chain around my neck. Twice I reached up and touched it just to reassure myself that it really was back. Now I could meet Aaron and Dynamike, open the cash box as if nothing had happened, and the members of the WHAM Agency could start the search for another three-legged buffalo.

9

By the time Aaron and Dynamike arrived at my house to help me count the money from the carnival, I was smooth and collected. And of course, I didn't even mention my lost-and-found-again key. That was way too embarrassing.

Oh, I wasn't dumb enough to think Allison would forget about it. In fact I was sure she'd blab about how her little sister had wrestled it off of me. But that wouldn't happen until Monday at school. That was a long way off. And maybe, just maybe, I'd have more exciting news than Allison did by Monday morning.

As soon as my buddies arrived, I picked up the cash box and we thundered down the stairs to the rec room where we sat on the carpet in a circle. I wanted to check out all those coins as fast as I could. But as I was unlocking the cash box, Aaron spoke up.

"I know it's going to be hard," he said, "but let's count up the profits really quickly without examining them. Then we can concentrate on checking each coin to see if there's another valuable one."

I started to protest, but stopped and sighed. I could use Aaron's help and I knew this was the only way my treasurer's report would get done this morning. We'd count first, and save our investigating for last, like dessert. "Okay," I said.

"Sure," Dynamike agreed. "But let's work fast."

As I dumped out the coins into a pile on the carpet, Aaron said, "I was talking to my dad about how I hoped we'd find another three-legged buffalo this morning. He thought the chances of us finding another rare coin were about as good as lightning striking twice in the same spot. But he watched me leave the house and I could tell he wished he was coming along."

I knew that Aaron's dad was probably right. Expecting more rare coins was pretty silly. But something inside me insisted that another lightning bolt was aimed straight at the WHAM Agency.

Without looking carefully at each coin, it was easy to count. We quickly separated everything into piles: pennies, nickels, dimes, quarters, and fifty-cent pieces. Then we worked separately, and when we finished one pile, we moved to another, counting, jotting down figures, and adding them up.

"Hey! None of that!" I said to Dynamike when I caught him examining one of the coins. "That comes later, remember?"

"Right," Dynamike said, looking sheepish as he dropped the coin into the heap.

It didn't take long, and we compared notes until finally we all came up with the same answer, $121.25. Of course, that's what Aaron had written down in the first place. That's why I liked his help. Aaron didn't make mistakes.

"Wow!" Dynamike said. "When this gets added to the checks and cash from the carnival, plus the money from the popcorn sale and the three-legged buffalo, it means student council has big bucks."

"Yeah, and the semester isn't over yet," I said. "I'll bet we set some kind of record." I wrote down the sum and put my report in the bottom of the cash box with a sigh of relief that it was done. Aaron and Dynamike looked at me expectantly. We hovered over the coins ready to pounce like cats on mice.

"Now, for the fun part," I said. "If coins are dated earlier than 1950, we'll pull them out and phone Mr. Bates. And let's save the nickels for last."

There was nothing interesting among the fifty-cent pieces, quarters, or dimes. But I didn't feel discouraged. My hopes weren't pinned on them. Our piles dwindled as we dropped the coins we'd examined back into the cash box. When there was nothing special among the pennies, either, I felt a little uneasy. Could it be that there were no valuable coins here?

Last of all, we looked at the nickels, one by one. I was feeling more and more discouraged with the dwindling heap, when Dynamike yelled, "Look! An Indian head nickel!"

Aaron and I leaned closer to him. "Darn," Dynamike said, as he peered closely at the coin. "This buffalo's got four legs."

Aaron took the coin and examined it. "But it's dated 1913. That's the first year the buffalo nickel came out. Even with all four legs, it may be valuable. Way to go, Dynamike! I'll call Dad."

Aaron had already started to scramble to his feet before I managed to grab his leg and pull him back down. "Wait!" I yelled.

Dynamike and Aaron both stared at me. "There may be more," I said. "Let's look at them all first and then call."

I guess I wanted lighting to strike not twice, but three or four times! So we went back to examining the pile of coins.

Almost immediately, Dynamike said, "Here's another one. A 1924 Indian head."

I thought to myself, Hurray for the WHAM Agency! This is Dynamike's lucky day. Then I looked at the coin I'd just picked up that was still in my hand. "Hey! Here's a 1916!"

"And this is a 1943 Jefferson," Aaron said, waving a coin and standing up. "I'm calling Dad right now."

This time I didn't try to stop him. While he was phoning, Dynamike and I checked out the remaining coins. Then we took all the coins up to the kitchen and inspected them once more, leaving our special ones out by themselves. I ran out to the garage to get Dad and I called Mom. By this time, Mr. Bates was on our doorstep. I had the feeling that he'd been sitting in his house with his coat zipped up just waiting around for a phone call.

We all sat around the table, as slowly and carefully, Mr. Bates inspected each of our four special nickels. "I can't believe this," he said. He put down his magnifying glass and stared at us open mouthed. "Each of these is valuable."

"Here." He handed the magnifying glass to Aaron. "If you look at the 1943 Jefferson nickel carefully, you'll see that the three in the 1943 is pressed over a two." He consulted his book. "In fine condition, it's worth $65. If it's extra-fine, it's worth $200."

Each of us took turns with the magnifier.

I looked up the 1924S Indian head in Mr. Bates's book while Aaron and Dynamike stared at it through the magnifying glass. "It says it's worth $14.50 in fine condition and $400 if it's extra fine," I reported. "I sure hope it's extra fine." I thumbed to another page. "And the 1913S is worth somewhere between $115 and $200."

"Now look up the 1916 nickel," Mr. Bates said. As he spoke, he handed it to Dynamike. "If you look closely at the 1916, you'll see that it has a double die strike."

I looked it up in the book. When I found it, I started to read the numbers, "twenty seven ..." I stopped. My hand started shaking so much it was hard to keep my finger in the right column. "Am I reading this right?" I asked.

I handed the book to Mr. Bates. His jaw dropped open before he finally said, "You're reading it right. If that nickel is graded extra fine, it's worth $2,700," Mr. Bates said. For a minute nobody spoke.

"We'll have to take all these to Mr. Jennings," I said.

"Right," Mr. Bates agreed, "and you'll have to be patient. It may take some time to grade them. He may even want to consult a colleague. A slight difference in grading can mean a lot of money. But the big question is, how did all these valuable coins end up being spent at your school carnival?"

"It can't be an accident," Aaron said. "My guess is that some kid has gotten into his parent's coin collection and is spending the nickels without realizing how valuable they are."

"Could be," I agreed. "Or it could be some adult who doesn't realize how much these coins are worth."

"But who?" Dynamike asked.

Aaron, Dynamike, and I stared at each other, and at exactly the same time, we all said, "The old man in the blue beret."

"What old man in the blue beret?" Mom asked.

We described the man we'd seen the night before. "The way he held onto that old coin purse made him look real suspicious," I said.

"It's certainly worth looking into," Dad said. "Did any of you happen to notice this old fellow when you were selling popcorn at the fair a couple of weeks ago?"

Aaron and Dynamike shook their heads. "At first I thought he looked a little familiar," I admitted. "But when I got a better look, I knew I hadn't seen him before. There were tons of people at the winter fair though. He could have been there and we just didn't see him. I think he's our number one suspect. In fact, he's our only suspect."

"I wish one of us had seen him at the popcorn sale," Dynamike said. "Because it's got to be somebody who came to the winter fair at the Elks' Club and to the school carnival. We got a valuable coin in each place."

"And it's got to be somebody in the neighborhood or connected to school," Aaron added. "Lots of folks from all over town were at the Elks' Club fair. But people wouldn't come clear across town just to attend a school carnival."

"You're right," I said, admiring Aaron's sleuthing skills.

"Maybe it's not the old guy in the blue beret," Dad said. "Maybe it's someone else. You boys were at the winter fair and spent the whole evening at the carnival. Can you think of anyone at all that you definitely saw in both places?"

"Lots of folks," I answered, and began to tick them off on my fingers. "Some of the teachers, Mr. Tobias, the principal, Chelsea and her grandmother, Mrs. Huffaker. Mrs. Carabell and her friend, Mrs. McCorkle."

"Doris McCorkle was there?" Mom asked.

"Yeah. In fact, she and Mrs. Carabell were both talking to the man in the blue beret. We tried to get through the crowd last night to meet him while he was with them, but he left. I was going to phone Mrs. Carabell today and ask the name of the old guy. I thought with an introduction from her, we could call or visit him and ask about the coins."

"And you could still do that," Mr. Bates said. "But your dad's right, Wink. The most likely person is someone you saw at both places."

"Do you know Mrs. McCorkle, Mom?"

"Only slightly. I've seen her a time or two with Mrs. Carabell. I know her husband died just a few months ago."

"Hey," I said. "I wonder if Mr. McCorkle was a coin collector?"

"That's a long shot," Dad said.

"Yeah, but I've got a weird feeling," I said, "a WHAMie in my stomach, and it's never wrong. We're on to something. I'm going to call up Mrs. Carabell and see what she knows about the man in the beret, and I'll ask about Mrs. McCorkle, too."

I grabbed my trusty notebook and pencil out of my back pocket. Then I looked up Mrs. Carabell's number in the phone book. I used the kitchen phone so that everyone could at least hear my half of the conversation. It fell very quiet after I dialed the numbers.

Some people would have been surprised to receive a phone call on Saturday morning from a kid asking a bunch of questions, but Mrs. Carabell seemed happy to talk. First, I asked what she knew about the old man in the blue beret.

"The gentleman is Andrew Wyatt," she said. As she talked, I began scribbling in my notebook. "He lives over on Sheridan Way, the same street where Doris lives, and he has two great-granddaughters at Hennessey School. One's in kindergarten and one's in first grade. He was bragging about them last night. He just got back on Sunday from a month-long trip to see England's castles. He promised to show me his slides one of these days."

While I kept scribbling in my notebook, I went right on with my interrogation. "You're sure Mr. Wyatt only got back from England on Sunday?" When I said that, I looked at the group seated around the table. Dynamike and Aaron both looked glum.

"Yes," she said firmly.

"Okay," I continued. "Now I have another question. It's about your friend, Mrs. McCorkle. Did her husband by any chance collect coins?"

"I don't know, but I'd be glad to call up Doris and ask. Is it important?"

"Very important," I said.

"All right. I'll phone her and then I'll call you right back."

While we waited around the phone, Aaron said, "Well, we can scratch the man in the blue beret off our list. Sounds like he was in England during the popcorn sale."

"Yeah," I said. "Mrs. Carabell was sure of that. He was just attending the fair to support his great-grandkids."

"The only lead we have left is Mrs. McCorkle," Dynamike said.

It fell quiet again while we all stared at the telephone.

Even though I was expecting it, when the phone finally did ring, I jumped.

"Wink," Mrs. Carabell said, "I don't know what this means, although I assume it has something to do with your WHAM Agency, but Doris said her husband, Angus, was a coin collector."

"Oh, wow!" I said, nodding wildly to the others gathered around me. "Would you call her back and ask Mrs. McCorkle if we could pay her a visit right away? It's really, really important."

Mrs. Carabell didn't waste a lot of time asking questions. She just said, "All right," and sounded excited and eager to help.

"Please call me right back," I said, "and if it's okay with her, we'll go right over. If you want to come, too, we'll pick you up before we go to Mrs. McCorkle's house."

Dad and Mr. Bates both nodded as I said this.

"Yes, I don't want to miss finding out what all this is about," she said. "I'll call you right back."

Mrs. Carabell quickly rang back and confirmed our meeting.

I was so excited, I forgot to ask exactly where Mrs. McCorkle lived.

"Better look up her address," Aaron's dad said. "We'll need to take two cars, and we might get separated driving over there."

In the phone book, I found a listing for Angus McCorkle at 7819 Sheridan Way and jotted the address down for Mr. Bates.

Within ten minutes, Mom, Dad, Mrs. Carabell, and I drove to Mrs. McCorkle's house in our car. Mr. Bates, Aaron and Dynamike followed us. As we drove I couldn't help thinking, if we had really discovered the source of the coins, that was good news for the WHAM Agency. We would have solved another case. But of course that meant we'd have to give the coins back. We'd probably even owe her for the one we already sold to the dealer after the popcorn sale. So the bad news was, our student council treasury might be about to take a big hit.

We parked and hurried to the front door where a puzzled Mrs. McCorkle let us all in.

"Dear, dear," she said. "I really wasn't expecting company. Please excuse the house."

There was nothing to excuse as far as I could see. Everything was neat as could be.

We sat down, and Mrs. Carabell made the introductions, ending by saying, "And you remember the boys you met at the school carnival."

"Oh, yes," Mrs. McCorkle said, smiling politely at me and then beaming at Aaron. "You're the young man who gave me the beautiful plant. I put it over there in the window where it can get plenty of light," she said, pointing to the little plant Aaron had won last night.

"The reason we're here," I explained, "is that we found a valuable coin spent at our popcorn sale at the winter fair. And some more coins were spent last night at the school carnival. You were at both places, and when we heard that your husband had been a coin collector, it occurred to us that you might be the one who had spent them."

"Oh, no," Mrs. McCorkle protested. "Mr. McCorkle was a numismatist. You're right about that. But he kept his coins in cases to protect them. And of course I wouldn't think of taking them out. I'm saving them for a rainy day," she explained, "in case there's an emergency."

I sighed, noticing that everyone else looked as glum as I felt. "Well, I'm sorry we bothered you, Mrs. McCorkle. It's just that when those nickels turned up at the carnival last night, I remembered you handing me some coins when you bought a bag of popcorn from me at the winter fair."

"Nickels?" Mrs. McCorkle repeated. "Did you say nickels?"

"Yes," I said. "Five valuable nickels have turned up so far."

"You know there were some nickels in a jewelry box where Mr. McCorkle kept his tie clips and cuff links. Because they weren't in cases, I didn't think they were special. When I came across them the other day, I dropped them in my coin purse."

"Do you remember how many there were?" I asked.

"Ten," Mrs. McCorkle responded quickly. "I remember thinking I'm not going to leave these here, they're worth fifty cents. And I dropped them in my purse."

We all sat there speechless staring at each other.

Mrs. Carabell recovered first. "Doris, do go get your purse," she said.

10

Mrs. McCorkle hurried back into the living room clutching her old handbag. She sat down in her rocker, unzipped the center section, pulled out a small black coin purse, and dumped the contents into her lap.

I saw Mr. Bates flinch. Even though I was new to this coin collection business, I knew what he must be thinking. Every nick and scratch on a coin reduces its value, and those valuable nickels had already been jiggling around with other coins for days now.

"I wonder if you might have a soft towel we could put these coins on?" Mr. Bates asked politely.

I watched him flinch again, as Mrs. McCorkle scooped the coins back into her coin purse and dropped them into her handbag again. "Of course. Of course." She scurried from the room to get a little embroidered guest towel, which she spread at one end of the dining room table.

As she dumped the coins onto the towel, we all gathered around, and Dynamike, Aaron, and I quickly picked out the nickels. Soon five of the ten coins, which had once been safely housed in Mr. McCorkle's velvet-lined jewel box, were resting on the towel at one end of the gleaming dining table.

Mom and Dad sat down on one side of the table while Mrs. McCorkle and Mrs. Carabell sat on the other. Mr. Bates sat at the head of the table with the towel spread in front of him. Dynamike, Aaron, and I stood behind him, hanging over his shoulders. He pulled out his magnifying glass and studied each of the nickels in turn.

Finally, Mr. Bates, announced, "You have some valuable coins here, Mrs. McCorkle." He stood and handed the magnifying glass to me, and I shared it with Aaron and Dynamike as we jostled close to each other, taking turns at examining each of the nickels.

"I'd recommend that you take these to a coin dealer and have their exact value determined," Mr. Bates continued.

Everyone started talking at once. Mrs. McCorkle kept looking from one to the other of us. She seemed very confused. Finally she said, "I guess I've come into a real windfall. You mean those nickels might be worth a lot?"

"Maybe hundreds," I said. She gasped and put her hand to her mouth. "If you'd like, the WHAM Agency would be happy to take these to a coin dealer for you and find out exactly how much they're worth." I told her. "We'd report back to you. Then you can decide if you'd like to sell or keep them."

"That's a wonderful idea, Doris," Mrs. Carabell reached out and took her friend's hand. "After all, the WHAM Agency helped me when my cat was lost. You remember me telling you about that. And they've helped you a great deal already. These young men are so clever. Without them, you'd have never known these coins were valuable."

"We've done business with a local coin dealer before," Aaron added, as if to reassure her. Then I watched his face suddenly cloud over. I realized that for the first time, Aaron, too, was realizing that student council would have to refund the money that Mr. Jennings had already given us.

"All right, boys, I'll leave this in your hands." Mrs. McCorkle disappeared for a bit, and we could hear her rummaging around in some drawers. She returned with a long, narrow white box that had once held a necklace. When she opened it, I saw two layers of soft cotton in it. She carefully spaced out the coins between the two cotton layers and handed the box to me.

We left right after that and took Mrs. Carabell home. As soon as we got back to our house, I called Mr. Jennings to tell him what was happening and to ask if we could show him the coins on Monday afternoon. He was quick to agree.

Right after school on Monday, Mom drove Dynamike, Aaron, and me to the coin shop where Mr. Jennings eagerly greeted us. He put the four nickels from the carnival and the five nickels we'd rescued from Mrs. McCorkle's purse on the blue velvet pad on his counter.

Carefully he examined each one through his jeweler's loupe. After each examination, he made some notes on his pad.

The four of us watched and waited. It seemed like forever, and I found myself staring at the minute hand on the wall clock, silently urging it forward.

"Well," Mr. Jennings said at last, "I hope your friend is willing to sell these. There are some very rare coins here, and I believe I have a collector who might be interested in them. Two of these coins could be extremely valuable."

"How much is extremely valuable?" I blurted out.

Mr. Jennings smiled. "Here's what I can offer." He pushed his notepad in front of us, and pointed at each of the figures with his pen as he explained.

"Both 1943P Jefferson nickels are extra fine and will sell for $200 each. One of the 1924S Indian heads is very fine and will sell for $150. The other is extra fine and will sell for $400. The 1937D three-legged buffalo should sell for $365. One of the 1913S Indian heads will sell for $195 and the other one for $200." The next two numbers on his pad were circled.

"It's the two 1916 double-die Indian heads that I want to get a second opinion on. I'd rate them as very fine. If I'm right, each one is worth $1,800."

"Oh, my gosh," I said.

Mr. Jennings took out his calculator and began punching in the numbers. "As you boys know, I pay 35 percent less than the list price. So if I confirm those values, I could offer you $3,451.50 for the nine coins."

My mother's eyes widened and she grinned at me, before Aaron, Dynamike, and I jumped in the air and exchanged high fives.

"Wow! That'll be a fortune to Mrs. McCorkle." Then, feeling a little sad in spite of myself, I added, "And of course, there's another $250 that we owe her from student council. I think that Mr. Doyle will want to pay it back now that we know who owned the coin we sold from the popcorn sale."

"I'm sure he will," my mother agreed.

Mr. Jennings said, "If you'd like, I could give you a receipt for these and keep the coins in our safe. I'll call my colleague and get a second opinion tomorrow. Then I'll phone you and make a firm offer."

Clutching the receipt in my hand as we drove back home, I said, "A lot depends on those two 1916 nickels. We'd better not tell Mrs. McCorkle a definite price until we hear from Mr. Jennings. I'd hate to disappoint her if the second opinion makes the amount go down."

"I think that's a good idea," Mom said. "You'll only have to wait a day, and then you'll be absolutely sure."

"Boy! It's going to be hard to wait," Dynamike said.

"And it'll be even harder for Mrs. McCorkle," I pointed out. "I'll phone her and tell her that we've taken them into the coin shop and that Mr. Jennings needs to consult with another dealer, but we'll be able to tell her how much the nickels are worth tomorrow. Then she'll know almost as much as we do."

"Good idea," Aaron said. "Investigators keep their clients informed."

"And you'd better phone Mrs. Carabell, too," Mom said. "She'll be dying of curiosity."

As I suspected, on Tuesday morning at school when I told Mr. Doyle what we'd discovered, he immediately wrote a check to Mrs. McCorkle for $250. I was sorry to see the amount in our treasury go down, and I hated the thought that Allison would never stop bragging about her fund-raiser idea, which was so much more successful than my popcorn sale, and teasing me about losing the money box key to her baby sister. But I was happy for Mrs. McCorkle, and I knew it was the right thing to do. Besides, with the success of the carnival and popcorn sale, even without the extra money from the coins, we still had a fat treasury balance.

When I got home from school that day, Mom was waiting with news. "Mr. Jennings phoned. He asked that you call him as soon as you got home."

I punched in the number of the coin shop, got Mr. Jennings on the phone, and then held my breath. He got right to the point. "The other coin dealer agrees with me about the condition of all the nickels but one. He rated the 1916 double die Indian head as extra fine, which increases its value by $900. That means I can offer you $4,036.50."

"Wow!" I said. "Wow! I'll let Mrs. McCorkle know right away, and I'll phone you back as soon as I talk with her."

I quickly phoned Aaron, Dynamike, Mrs. McCorkle, and Mrs. Carabell. I didn't give details, just said we needed to meet. Aaron and Dynamike immediately biked to my house, I climbed on my bike, and the three of us sped over to Mrs. McCorkle's. As she'd promised me over the phone, Mrs. Carabell had driven over there and was already waiting to hear the news. "He'll pay you $4,036.50," I announced.

The women gasped and my buddies grinned.

"Dear, oh dear, oh dear," Mrs. McCorkle kept saying. "I can hardly believe it! Of course I'll sell him the nickels. It will be wonderful to have all that money tucked away in my little savings account. I can't thank you enough!" There were tears in her eyes.

"The WHAM Agency is always ready to help," Aaron said.

She smiled through her tears at the three of us. "Lucy told me that she gave each of you engraved business cards for your investigating agency as a reward when you found her missing cat," Mrs. McCorkle said. "I didn't know what to get you for the help you've given me, so when I was in town today, I stopped at the bank and got three shiny silver dollars." She took the dollars out of her purse and handed one to each of us.

I felt a little twinge of disappointment and thought that maybe we should consider raising our rates.

She took the dollars out of her purse and handed one to each of us.

"Thank you very much," we each said. Quickly, I looked at the date on mine. I noticed that Dynamike and Aaron were doing the same thing.

Watching us, Mrs. McCorkle laughed. "I'm afraid they're only worth a dollar."

We stood up then, ready to leave, when I said, "Oh, I almost forgot. Here's a check from our student council." I reached into my pocket and handed it to her. "You see, we sold the first buffalo nickel that you spent at our pop-corn booth before we knew who it belonged to. It's only fair that we return the profit to you."

"No, no, no," Mrs. McCorkle insisted. "You take that check right back to your sponsor and ask him to tear it up. Tell him I insist that your student council keep that money. Consider it a reward. After all, if you boys hadn't investigated and tracked me down, I'd have spent those ten nickels and never been the wiser."

I stood there hesitating, my hand still holding out the check. "Are you sure?"

"I'm very sure," she said.

"Gee, thanks. Thanks a lot." I put the check back into my pocket, and tucked my silver dollar in with it for safe keeping.

"Thank you very much, Mrs. McCorkle," Aaron said, shaking her hand.

As Dynamike shook her hand, he said, "We'll count

you among the satisfied customers of the WHAM Agency."

Outside the house, as we climbed back on our bikes, I said. "Well, that closes the Case of the Three-Legged Buffalo." I threw my leg over the bike, and as I pedaled off, I turned to my buddies and asked, "I wonder what mystery we'll solve next ..."